Scribblers' Pen
A Collection of Short Stories

Pegswood Hub

Creative Writers

This book is set in Calibri 11pt

Front cover photograph by Martin Booth

Copyright © 2017 Pegswood Community Hub Creative Writers

All rights reserved.

ISBN-13: 978-1978165564
ISBN-10: 1978165560

DEDICATION

We would like to dedicate this book to the staff and volunteers at Pegswood Community Hub who work so hard for their local community.

We would also like to dedicate the book to Dave Telfer, who sadly died earlier this year. A writer, singer and performer, Dave was a member of the Writing Group and Drama Group for several years.

He will be much missed.

CONTENTS

Emma-jane Anderson

    A Moment's Reflection………………………….185

Kate Booth

    Life Long Love……………………………………….17

    Water At Every Turn………………………………21

    On the Equinox, Super Moon and Eclipse……29

    Heaven on Earth……………………………………37

    The Smell Of Success……………………………..65

    Ellie's Fairy Wood…………………………………..98

    Wilbur Loved Books So Much………………….127

    Bursting Bubbles………………………………….180

Martin Booth

    Memories……………………………………………41

    Earth, Wind, Fire and Water……………………70

    I Like The Dead…………………………………….92

    He Kinda Liked The Feelin'… ………………….114

    Cooking With The Dark Arts……………………130

    Vegetable Stew……………………………………142

    If Only… ……………………………………………152

    Magma……………………………………………..170

    Worship Me! ………………………………………184

Daniel Brown

    Set You Free……………………………………………….61

    Jack Who Had Two Faces……………………….82

    Cabinet Pussy-Cat………………………………………118

    Bigg Night Out…………………………………………….137

    Extracts from the Pages of the

        Dark Lord's Confession………………..174

Linda Jobling

    A Day At The Seaside……………………………….45

    What Happened To Jasper……………………108

    The Ring………………………………………………………164

Oonah V Joslin

    Never Trust A Talking Cat………………………12

    All Gardens Have Their Secrets………………19

    Nellie's Moss Monster……………………………..26

    Garden Acrostic………………………………………..31

    Saint Swithin's Day…………………………………..35

    The Dispensary…………………………………………57

    About Time! …………………………………………….74

    Just A Phage He's Going Through……………136

    Forever Berries……………………………………….149

    Woodshed Live……………………………………….161

    A Bit of Bad Weather…………………………….167

Margaret Kerswell

> The Hub………………………………………………10
>
> Fishing…………………………………………….…20
>
> Haibun……………………………………………….27
>
> The Piano In The Woods…………………….32
>
> A Quote and 100 Words……………………..69
>
> Altar Of Bones……………………………………81
>
> Daughters of Eden…………………………….102
>
> A Silky Special Dress…………………………129
>
> Sleeping Beauty: A Fantasy………………..135
>
> "No-one Under The Age Of Forty…" ……….145
>
> Cyclops, Maze, Pandora's Box………………154

Harry Lane

> Reflection……………………………………………11
>
> Butterfly……………………………………………..25
>
> Autumn……………………………………………….34
>
> The Sixties…………………………………………..38
>
> Thud……………………………………………………52
>
> Toward The Light………………………………..77
>
> Midnight Sun……………………………………..112
>
> Character…………………………………………..133
>
> Good Morning, Geraldine……………………146

Dave Telfer

Lara's Big Day..187

Author Biographies...190

What Is Pegswood Community Hub?...................193

Authors' Notes...

The stories and poems in this book are examples of the work that the Pegswood Writing Group has produced over the past four years. We meet on a Wednesday morning at Pegswood Community Hub to write, talk and drink coffee.

The inspiration for the works vary widely, from those written to a common theme for everyone, to those the writers felt they just had to write. Some are funny, some serious and some are very personal.

Authors write stories which interest them and hope that others will enjoy them as well; that is the case with this anthology. We hope that you will find something to enjoy, something to make you think and something which will bring a lump to your throat. If we have done this, we have succeeded in what we set out to do. Enjoy.

Poems

The Hub

By Margaret Kerswell

Fun and games, on family nights

Tom in a dress, he looks alright

Our favourite dame, you'll be glad you came

Panto next year will be fun once again

Quiz and a pint, you can enjoy

If you come to quiz night, be you girl or boy

The question master? Tom's the name

Jokes and knowledge is his game

Feeling hungry? Something nice to eat?

Sumptuous Supper is a treat

Anne's culinary skills put to the test

We wonder what you'll like the best.

Arty, crafty or simply laughter

It doesn't matter what you're after

With groups galore, you're sure to find

The perfect way to spend your time

So see you there? You won't be lonely

At Pegswood Hub, the one and only.

Reflection

By Harry Lane

When I was born

The world was green

Youth flowed over the land

Skies were clear

The air bright

And I was not afraid

Time has passed

I'm not so sure

The skies overhead have turned grey

The road ahead is not so straight

And, I'm afraid I'll lose my way

Never Trust a Talking Cat

By Oonah V Joslin

Ever since that cat arrived

my life's gone down the chute.

To start with he demanded

a pair of shiny boots.

I tried to state the obvious;

I was the one in charge

but he stood up on his hind legs

his eyes all bright and large,

he put his forepaws on his waist

and whiskered his disdain,

I'll need a coat and trousers too.

Cats do not like the rain.

His stolid and unflinching look

crumpled my resolution.

To give him what he wanted

seemed the easiest solution.

When he started poaching pheasants;

taking presents to the king

I thought *Oh good! I'm rid of him*

You know -- it's a cat thing.

But not a bit of it. This cat

had hatched a plan you see

and part of it involved a bit

of subterfuge and me.

The Royals had a daughter

a bit plain -- a bit rotund,

for whom it seemed no suitor

suitable had yet been found

and Puss, that's what I called him,

fancied a life of luxury

and decided in his scheming way

that she should marry me.

So while I was skinny-dipping

he purloined all my clothes,

flagged down the princess' carriage

and she said: *Here put on those*

and made her footman take his off.

She said I looked quite fine.

Then she drove me to the palace

and ordered meat and wine.

I don't recall what happened next

but it seems I am engaged.

That furtive and rapacious cat

had my whole life story staged.

It's the night before the wedding

and I've never been more sure

her father the King's an imbecile

and the princess is a whore.

I know I can't go through with it.

Marry? I'd rather kill her.

I was never meant to be a prince.

I'm content as a simple a miller.

I am writing this for you today

'cos I won't be here tomorrow.

Don't mess with talking animals.

They'll only bring you sorrow.

Don't be like me, so innocent!

Talking cats aren't at all cute.

They're malevolent, maleficent.

Life Long Love

By Kate Booth

When relationships work, Time will not alter them.

So………your courtship is the time

When you learn about the real person that you are attracted to.

Each a lunch time sandwich, or drink on a date,

Measures their smile and humour, and their loves and hates.

Talking lets you compare your values, and learn about their tastes,

It makes time and it tests their ability to listen,

As well as yours to do the same, so you both have the chance to learn.

Caring is only possible if sharing comes naturally:

The sharing of common interests and the joy of victories won.

Problems shared may not just be halved,

The process of discussing and testing different and new approaches,

Courting helps you to see the world through someone else's eyes.

Love comes when you find a mate of your type.

A gentle soul, who is kind, and considerate,

Showing you consideration and being honest with their views.

Touching your very soul with a pertinent word or observation,

Giving you goose pimples with that breathy kiss on your neck.

In passing years there may be significant changes,

Time will change us all,

But health changes are those that challenge us the most,

Particularly the ones we love.

Everyone needs to be supported by a caring partner,

To hear their fears or to share their courage and optimism.

Love is a deep blessing, to be acknowledged,

 And spoken out loud, every day.

Time will make us wrinkle, but love and life-long team work will smooth them out.

Marriage

All Gardens Have Their Secrets

By Oonah V Joslin

from a Painting at The Hub

Against the whitewashed cottage walls
amidst the cobbles in a circle grew
purple flowers in spring and orange bonnets.

Oh the show of it
among the feathery fennel green,
its yellow tops spoked like the sun.

And in the autumn of their days,
my grandparents were our lanterns
and we were their sunshine for a day.

We picked some silver pennies of honesty
as we'd picked the bluebells in spring.
In granny's garden, parsley grew, and everlasting flowers.

There's such a thing as too much honesty,
tangled tendrils, scattered seed.
Fennel can be a bitter weed.

Fishing

By Margaret Kerswell

The wind picks up

Blows harder still

As rain clouds darken

Show their will

The gently lapping water

Starts lapping twice as hard

The colour grows much darker

Not like the bright postcard

The wind does pick up stronger

You start to feel a chill

Blowing o'er the water

Through trees and over hill

The day that once was sunny

Turns chill, dark and wet

And will we ever catch a fish?

Well, that's anybody's bet

Water At Every Turn

By Kate Booth

The sea speaks in a Kingly voice.

It has run its course and pounded the rocks,

The water heaves back, clawing pebbles across its mates.

Retreating water undercuts the next wave,

Pushing it higher, adding to the incoming flow.

The weight of water landing has many voices.

Crashing of a massive form with its choral roar,

Leaving trails of foam, that pop and gurgle.

The regular tidal rhythm of incoming and retreating waves

Can be calming and sleepy, on a 'small wave' day.

Bringing in gentle, whispering ripples

Wetting, caressing, and feeding the barnacles and anemones.

Splashing fresh water into the rock pools.

 Or just trickling through the pebbles,

Seeping silently, in dribbles and drips.

The winds conduct the change in tones.

Waves grow higher and drop harder.

Crashing crescendos, reaching further up the shore.

Sand is dragged along to new venues,

Pebbles squeal as they grind to a halt.

Final words are tossed up as spray, which flies out to wet cliff faces.

Walkers are wet, and spectators refreshed.

Soft rocks and cliffs are undercut,

Making areas collapse and slump.

Felled by a timeless stroke.

The pitch of the coming storm rises, having travelled from afar;

This fading hurricane makes waves even higher.

These monsters are driven by a pregnant sea.

Pushing up the crashing waves, and adding thunder to each break.

Spray reaches higher, and the surges push in

Filling every crevice and crack.

With nowhere left to go, salt water floods the surrounding land.

Air is saturated with water vapour.

Rising to condense as clouds, but rubbing air particles builds up the static.

Flash, pause and then the CRASH of the thunder, earthing to the ground

Pattering drops of rain, so fresh water now falls.

Not salt but pure fresh to drink, and to raise the crops.

Perhaps the sky is too bright but the water trickles and drains out of sight.

Seeping is silent, but gravity is relentless.

Naturally, Down is non- negotiable, only the speed varies.

Mountain sides bear the scars of this losing battle.

Worn and broken by the many forms of water.

Deep valley gouges, where a glacier once passed .

Rocks picked up like teeth, scouring rock over rock.

Dumping debris as dams, in these U shaped valleys.

Melted water is just as savage; cutting V shaped valleys as they go.

Rushing head long over rocks, waterfalls take water down down down.

Shouting relentlessly; in a steady roar.

The water dissolves many rocks, and minerals.

Carried away in seeping dribbles

Their soluble bodies are then rebuilt with steady drips.

Stalactites hang on and hang down,

Drips have more to give, Drip Drip

A large plinth of stalagmites carrying their stony cargo.

Deep caves in the ground keep them safe.

Cracks widen and caves evolve around rock falls.

Crumbling back to darkness.

A new home for many animals,

 Being blind is no problem, but sensitive to sound, vibrations, taste and more.

Bats share the space, to roost and rest safely.

Leaving to hunt, in the wider sky.

The streams converge and coalesce;

Becoming heavier at every turn.

Gouging out at its outer bends,

Sowing sediment on the inner turns.

This snake–like procession is waters' trade mark; no matter where it flows.

The wider the stream becomes the longer its' twisting waves.

Across the Universe water has left its mark.

On the Moon or Mars it behaved in the same fashion.

A recognisable signature we can read millions of miles away.

Destructive and creative, depositing, is the nature of water.

O who is glory in the shapeless maps?

Butterfly

By Harry Lane

Fractured light through chequered gauze

Tumbled flight o'er chamomile

The Nellie's Moss Monster

By Oonah V Joslin

Nellie's Moss monster sleeps the winter long

Her reedy mane defies the dark and frost.

The warmth of first spring sun and bright bird song,

And sap that rises through the bark, the lust

Of frogs and toads that stir the lakes

At the full moon of March is all it takes.

She wakes up to the sound of honking geese

Visitors' feet, cars crossing the bridge.

Cameras click and she has all she needs,

For it's on admiration that she feeds.

HAIBUN

By Margaret Kerswell

Sat in the car with three children, cruising at seventy miles per hour on the motorway can be an interesting experience, to say the least. With conversations covering everything from toileting matters to the weather, it's certainly an education.

On one long journey my two youngest had fallen asleep, this gave Andrew and me a chance to talk to Peter (our eldest), without the incessant questions from the gallery.

The conversation soon turned to the dreaded subject of 'school', my eldest pretty much views the 'S' word as swearing - he hates it; in fact, if we were to say he never had to go back there, we'd make him eternally happy. Although we have always encouraged and supported him as much as we can wherever possible, he has little to no confidence where school is concerned.

However we have for years heard from his teachers about how quick he is at learning, especially in subjects such as science, maths and history, with their only wish that he would get more of his knowledge on to paper.

Again though on this journey, as the world whizzed past we were destined to have the conversation about how he 'couldn't do it', how he 'felt useless' and how he didn't see the point.

"I just can't do it, mam," he said in a slightly huffy sounding voice.

"You can Peter," was my reply, as I turned as much as possible so I could see his face.

"But I'm not very good at it," he said.

"That doesn't matter, it's the fact that you keep trying that counts, plus if you keep persevering you'll get it right eventually," I encouraged.

"Yeah but in the meantime, I'm stupid," came his response.

"You're not stupid mate, you're learning, no-one knows everything, we all need to learn stuff." I tried not to sound totally exasperated.

"Even you?" he questioned.

"Yes, even me. When I first started drawing I couldn't do it very well, but I'd sit for hours and practise. Every time it didn't go right I'd start again. In fact I'm still learning! The point is I'm persevering. I won't give up, try, try and try again, even when things seem to be going against you, they'll come right in the end."

Peter looked at me thoughtfully.

"OK," he said, "I'll try a bit harder, but will you still help me sometimes?"

"Of course we will bud, that's what we're here for."

With the other two stirring the conversation petered out, as familiar questions started;

"Are we there yet?"

"When's dinner?"

"Can we stop soon?"

Ahhhh the joys of being a mam……..

Travelling the road

Of life, growing up is hard

At speed when you're young

On the Equinox, Super Moon and Eclipse...

By Kate Booth

Oh glorious symmetry...
A mathematician's destiny
Curving orbits of massive planets
Observed and recorded by
Thinking man as he has evolved,
His day ruled by light and dark
As we revolve around the sun.

Night and day the heat,
Cold in the shade without the sun.

Generations pass,
Learning to live with the cycles, the patterns,
Watching their world grow, glorious plants and grazing animals.
Passing down ideas,
Building on learning, passed down before.

Some ideas are reassessing,
Parents and family help us move around...
The first stroke of a hand,
A gentle hug in their arms.
Hearing their words, forming ideas in your mind.

Who first thought that thought?
Why?
How did that get discovered and when?

What made those steps in discovery follow on?
Oral tradition, to images of meaning,
Shapes in development.
Rote learning to the written word, to
Hieroglyphs and pictograms
Diagrams with descriptions.
Numbers to describe patterns
To be analysed and evaluated.

Shapes of relationships…

Garden Acrostic

By Oonah V Joslin

Geese fly south, a honking

Arrowhead. Overhead I hear wings.

Robin eats the apple core. Sings 'more'.

Damp composting worms find

Eden; grown and tangled in a day.

Next door's cat is never far away

The Piano in the Wood

By Margaret Kerswell

The piano lay quiet

Deep in the wood

The soldier approached it

And silently stood

It made him feel sad

Like no-body cared

The feeling was eerie

With no building, there

No seats for a crowd

To hear music so sweet

As the soldier walked forward

Hear the beat of his feet

He reached out his hand

And touched ivory cool

He couldn't sit down

For there was no stool

He proceeded to play

The notes ringing clear

It was just a shame

There's no audience here

Autumn

By Harry Lane

Spring's laughter

Summer's glory

And following behind came Autumn

No fanfare here

No herald to announce the coming of this season

The bright promise of Spring

The brilliant blaze of Summer

This approach was different

It came with measured step

And gentle solemn promise

Autumn - It came wreathed in gold and brown

Bearing quiet dignity

To preserve the past and guard the future

Autumn - Season of nostalgia

Of sweet backward glances and silent tears

Wrapped in warm melancholy

Autumn - Winter's first embrace

And Summer's last sigh

Autumn

Saint Swithin's Day

By Oonah V Joslin

Yesterday was St Swithin

and yes there was some cloud

except for when the sun came out

or it rained down heaven's hard;

except for when the weather turned,

changed its mind and turned again

and that time when the sun broke

through the middle of the rain.

It was warm until the wind blew up

then it got a wee bit nippy

but still, it was a lovely day

and everyone was happy

since we don't have a climate here

there is no reason why

we shouldn't have November

in the middle of July.

Heaven on Earth

By Kate Booth

I am lying in my warm comfortable bed.

There is no pain, what bliss.

There is just sinking, relaxing, and thoughtful acceptance.

The dappled light is occasionally broken by birds flying past the window.

The gentle breeze brings in fresh clean air, washed by the heavy rain last night.

Breathing calmly in and out makes me sink in the duvet, and my eyes shut.

If I could see this moment it would be the swirling colours of a rainbow.

It smells of the flowers and freshly washed soil in the garden.

There is also the smell of warm bread and chocolate.

Then I feel my soul mate, gently kiss and caress my forehead. My moment is complete.

I feel so grateful.

And sink completely into deep sleep…

The Sixties

By Harry Lane

Summer came sweet and we met her fair

Levis and Wranglers and long flowing hair

Music was different – it gave us the Cream

Heavy, progressive – protest was seen.

Dylan and Bayez to turn the tide:

Did Dylan really have 'God on his side'?

Hippies with beads and flowers in their hair

'Let's go to San Francisco', love is waiting there.

Then came the Mini, the car and the skirt,

Looking good in a cheesecloth shirt.

Gangs of lads and smiling lasses

Drinking pints of Tartan out of thick chunky glasses.

Holidays abroad with discos and dances

Long hot nights and holiday romances.

Thanks for the freedom, the love and the colour,

The song, the music that sounds like no other.

It sets us on high, it lifts us above,

All you need is a 'Whole lotta love'.

Thanks for the sun, the summer, the friends.

Thanks for giving us the days that never end.

So when I look back and take it all on board,

I'd like to say thanks to 'My Sweet Lord.'

Stories

Memories

By Martin Booth

"What the hell are you wearing?"

Colin looked down at himself, standing in a comfortable sitting room. "Er, I was sorting out some old clothes and I found these..."

Annabel, who had been checking emails on her iPad, put down her wineglass on the side table and adjusted her spectacles. "I thought I might be seeing things," she said, "but sadly, no". She paused and made the pretence of thinking. "Maybe I need another glass of red?"

"Oh come on, it's not too bad." Colin sucked in his stomach as far as he could. "You used to fancy me in these in the old days!"

"Yes, darling, but we were both a lot younger in the old days and nowhere near as wise."

Colin sat down on the armchair opposite his wife. There was a silence for several minutes. Annabel took another sip of wine and peered at her husband over the top of her reading glasses. "You're sulking now, aren't you?"

"No!"

"That is a definite sulk, Colin." Annabel put her glass down again and looked at him. "Look, I'm sorry... it was just a bit of a shock, that's all, seeing you in... those." She gestured with her hand. "It's not as if you've even got a bike now!"

Colin sat in the chair, trying to hold his stomach in but eventually he had to relax in order to breathe. "You used to wear this stuff as well... looked bloody gorgeous in it, too!"

Annabel gave a little smile. "Oh, I remember... you used to look pretty good yourself."

Colin leaned forwards in the chair, then sat back to stay... comfortable. "Remember those bike rides, darling? We thought nothing of a hundred miles in a day."

His wife put down the iPad next to the wine glass and sat back. "Oh, I remember. Camping by the seaside, laying in that ridiculous tent listening to the waves on the rocks."

"Aye, and remember when we stayed in that tepee thing for a laugh?"

Annabel giggled, a warm sound in the cosy suburban lounge. "Oh yes, and it collapsed halfway through the night because the guy who owned it didn't know how to put it up properly!" She leaned forwards and took another sip of wine. "They were happy days, before the kids and commitments."

He nodded. "Yes. It was a sad day when we sold the bikes to help pay for the car."

"True," said Annabel, "but as a busy mother I have to say it was a lot easier moving two kids and their stuff around in a car than on the back of a pushbike."

"I know." Colin carefully got up and went into the kitchen to get a wine glass and the bottle. Topping up his wife's glass, he poured himself a generous measure and sat back down. Annabel looked at him. "Don't be silly... come and sit over here."

He got up again and lowered himself gently down on the sofa next to his wife. Maybe the cycle shorts *were* a little too tight...

"I was thinking..."

Annabel smiled. "Isn't that the phrase that's meant to really worry your partner?"

Colin smiled. "OK. I was thinking... maybe I... we... should get some more bikes? I mean, the kids have left home and it would do us good to get out... you know, bit of exercise?"

"Darling, if I want to go a hundred miles now, I will use the car or I will take the train."

"Exercise?"

Annabel sighed. "Colin, I go to the gym twice a week and I swim. Anyway, I doubt I'd fit into my Lycra anymore..."

A silence filled every corner of the room as Colin digested what his wife had said. "So you've still got your cycle outfit as well, then?"

"Er, yes, it's in a case on top of my wardrobe."

It was Colin's turn to put down his glass. "So you kept your cycle shorts and top as well, and then made fun of me when I tried mine on."

"Oh come on, darling," said Annabel, "it was meant in fun. Anyway, I was a trim size 14 in those days... I'm afraid I'm a little bigger now. They wouldn't fit."

Colin looked down at the thin Lycra, stretched over his stomach. Time had not been kind to either of us, he thought, looking at the small white strands of elastic cracking on the black fabric as the usually tight fitting material perished. Another strand parted before his eyes. "I did used to like the feeling of this fabric," Colin said quietly, his head still down. When he looked up, he realised that Annabel was looking at him intently with a secretive smile on her face. "I know," she replied quietly, so that Colin couldn't hear, "so did I."

Colin stood up and sighed. "Oh well, I suppose I'll go and take this stuff off."

Annabel stood as well and took her husband by the arm. "Oh, I wouldn't be in so much of a hurry, darling." She grinned and stood on her tiptoes to kiss him. "Come on, let's see if I can still squeeze a size 16 me into a size 14 cycle outfit!"

A Day at the Seaside

By Linda Jobling

I sat in the large, well-polished pew that over the years had taken on the shape of a backside from the hours of sitting and listening to the boring sermons I had to endure. They were all the same: 'you must not swear or be envious of your friends, never steal, never be jealous etc. etc.' I was so bored and the sermon always ended the same. Somehow or another we would all end up in hell if we didn't do all these things. Well, I had already overheard a conversation about the preacher and his antics, so there was no way he was going to heaven.

"Who cares?" I thought. "I just want to go to the seaside."

I looked around the small Wesleyan chapel at the damp and peeling paint where water had seeped in for many a month. Such an eerie place that always seemed to me to be cold. The kneelers so carefully stitched in the "Band of Hope" on a Saturday morning were showing signs of wear and tear from all the kneeling and praying. I sat and sat. "Oh God! How long was this Minister going to go on for?" All I wanted to do was go to the seaside. I tried to divert my thoughts again, watching the pigeon through the glass window, flying to and fro with bits of twig and settling in the old yew tree outside.

My thoughts were shattered when the last hymn was announced. "Number 232 in your hymn book, 'Onwards Christian soldiers marching on to war'." What the hell was this all about? I wasn't a soldier and I certainly didn't want to go to war. On went the hymn, with Mary Williams singing like a cat being strangled and Ivor Williams her husband trying to sing tenor. He didn't half think he could sing.

"AAAAmen."

Thank goodness it was all over. All I needed to do now was to take my little red book to show my attendance at Sunday School and I would have enough 'ticks' to go on the trip. Gaynor, my sister, and I had attended every Sunday apart from two when we both had the chicken pox. We should be alright. We walked up the isle to the 'big seat' one by one as our names were called out. "Well done," Mr Jones the minister said, "there will be a place for you on the bus to Aberystwyth next month. We will be going from the 'top of the road' by the shop. You must be there on time or the bus will have to go without you. "No chance," I thought to myself, "I haven't sat here Sunday after Sunday listening to you..." Miss the bus? No chance.

The three weeks dragged on, until the morning of the big day arrived. It didn't start too good either. Gaynor was crying that she had a pain in her belly and I had to take my baby sister Joy to our Grandmothers. Mother placed Joy in the large blue pushchair, I could hardly see over the handle, I was so short. Off I went with this screaming baby up the road to my Grandmothers, passing Rosie's door on the way. Out she came, with a face like vinegar, to hear what the noise was all about. Not even a fly could pass her door without her seeing it.

"It's Joy," I said. "She will be alright in a minute. I'm just taking her up to Nanny's," I shouted. Waddling across the road she came in her lisle stockings and well-worn slippers with a pompom on the front. She peered over the pushchair.

"I'm in a hurry" I said. "I am going on the trip today". What I felt like saying was "shut up and go away or I'll miss the bus." So I tried very hard not to be cheeky - she might tell the Minister and I might not get on the bus after all. I ran as fast as I could the rest of the way with Joy's cries getting louder. Nanny was by the door waiting for me in her cross-over flowered apron and her hair tied back in a bun. She always looked lovely to me and I loved her very much. Her wrinkled face broke into a smile when she saw us. Her hands were a great fascination to me. Her skin was thin and transparent with long blue veins crisscrossing.

"Oh what is the matter with Joy," she said in a kind voice, as she picked Joy from the pushchair. "Come, come you'll be alright," she said as she cuddled her. I took off as soon as I could.

"Wait, wait," she shouted, "I have got something for you." O Holy moley what now? I know I'm going to miss the bus.

"Here's something for you, get yourself and Gaynor an ice-cream." "Thanks Nanny," I said, running down the path, trying to put the shiny sixpence in my coat pocket, twisting my feet on the gravel as I picked up speed. With my sandals full of gravel I kept running, forgetting the pain until I arrived home. People had already been collected at 'the top of the road'.

"Aren't you coming on the bus?" Phoebe the milk called.

"Yes, we'll be there in a minute," I shouted, now running faster than I thought possible.

Gaynor was still crying when I arrived back. "We won't be able to go now," I started shouting and crying at the top of my voice.

"There's always something wrong with Gaynor. Make her stop crying," I screamed.

"Stop being cheeky or you will stay at home. I have had enough of this. Both of you go upstairs, until you have calmed down," mother said in a very harsh voice. That is where we stayed for what seemed an hour until she called us down again. We could see all the other children heading for the 'top of the road'. I was desperate, so after some persuading Gaynor to take an Asprin, we set off, dressed in our Sunday clothes with our hair tied up in ringlets, and four red-rimmed eyes from crying.

Mother had packed a fresh loaf, a large lump of ham and some of the fresh butter that had been churned a few days before, two towels and two knitted red bathing costumes that had once been my Grandfather's jumper. We had helped her undo the jumper and wash the wool. Mother had taken weeks to do them with a pattern from the Woman's Weekly, finishing them just in time. Nothing she ever knitted fitted properly. We had never managed to get our head through any jumper she had knitted and she always seemed to be running out of wool. Then she used to add another colour around the neck. "Never mind," I thought; she was taking us on a trip today that's all that mattered to me. What we endured to go on this trip was unbelievable. We had slept all night with long rags in our hair to get ringlets that were by now getting on my nerves hanging down each side of my face.

It was a warm day and the sun was shining. The bus lurched to a stop. Mother got in to the front of the queue to get the best seat.

"You can't sit there," Alice shouted. "I was here first and I want that seat." "Well I'm not moving," Mother announced.

"Mam it doesn't matter," I begged. "Let's just sit anywhere."

"No I won't. I want the front seat and I'm staying here." All three of us squashed into the seat.

"Has everyone got a seat now?" the driver shouted. "Sit down, the bus is about to start". The bus wound its way around the bends throwing us around as it went under 'bont bell'.

"Stop the bus!" mother shouted at the driver. "Gaynor is sick." Oh God what now? I was getting fed up with her. The driver pulled to the side and indeed Gaynor was very sick.

"You should have given her some 'Kwells' before you started," Alice shouted from four seats behind.

"How was I to know she was going to be sick?" my mother answered at the top of her voice. Everything settled down for a while, Gaynor as white as a sheet and not enjoying the trip that we both longed for, for such a long time.

The bus carried on winding its way past this farm and that farm. "Oh there's Cilcwm," said one.

"There's the Fron," shouted another. Everyone was happy. Through all the little villages we went when a blood curdling shout came from the back of the bus.

"John feels sick, can you stop the bus?" Annie Jones shouted.

"What the hell? We'll never get there," I thought. The sea will have gone, I won't ever see it. The bus came to another grinding halt, out John went and he was sick on the side of the road, but we had managed to get about halfway. The rest of the journey went without a hitch. The other children on the bus were consuming pop and sweets and crisps at an alarming rate, but we had nothing as Gaynor was feeling sick.

I had seen pictures of the sea in my books, but I had no idea what it would look like and imagined that it was just like the lake at home. We had read stories at Sunday School about children who lived over the sea. I just could not wait to see it. We arrived at the top of the hill that drops steeply down to Aberystwyth.

"The sea, the sea!" mother announced: she had seen it first from the front of the bus.

"Where?" everyone shouted at once.

"There," mother pointed. How disappointed was I that it just looked like the sky.

"That's not the sea, mum," I said. "The sea has waves... it says so in my book."

"You'll see the waves when we get down to the shore," she replied. "You must wait for me to get a deckchair from the man on the prom and then you can take your shoes and socks off and go for a paddle. Are you listening?" She glared at me. "If you don't behave today, I'll tell your father tonight and you won't come again."

"Yes, mam," I replied, knowing I would get a smack if I didn't listen. I was used to those over the years: I normally wouldn't behave and was subjected to at least one a day. They didn't hurt so I didn't really care how many I had.

The driver opened the door of the bus to a mass exodus of Sunday School children. Heeding our mothers' advice we took our socks and shoes off and headed into the sea for a paddle. John, on the other hand, ran in fully clothed and fell in, Annie running down the beach for all she was worth in case he drowned. He spent the rest of the day in his pants and that was a great amusement to us all.

Gaynor was now feeling better and mother had acquired her deckchair. She was sitting cutting the bread and making sandwiches that we devoured with great relish. Bellies full, we put the large towel around us and managed to change into our bathing costumes. The pattern from the Woman's Weekly must have gone around the village as most of the girls had the same bathing costume varying in colour form black to purple stripes.

"Look! There's the donkeys coming up the beach," Gaynor exclaimed. "Can we have a ride on one?" we both pleaded. Mother pulled out her red leather purse. "I am only able to pay for you to go on the donkey or an ice cream, but you can't have both. You please yourself which one you want." We both chose to go for a ride on the donkey.

"This is Ned and this is Billy," the donkey man informed us. I was helped onto Ned and my sister Gaynor sat on Billy. Ned decided he had had enough and would not move: no amount of coaxing or pulling would shift him. Then he began to kick. The donkey man (I think his name was George) took me off the donkey and waited until the others came back and I was taken for a ride up the sands on my own. I didn't think much of it. I realised I had wasted my money and an ice cream would have been much better. The donkey was stinking! What with the flies and the stinking donkey, I did not enjoy the ride at all.

The sun was burning my skin so my mother covered my back and face in olive oil. "This will help," she said, but it didn't. Out came the calamine lotion, so I was covered from head to toe in the white stuff and looked rather like a ghost playing in the sand. Just as we were packing to get back on the bus, we heard this music.

"It's the ice cream van," Johnny shouted. All the children ran towards it clutching their money. We did not ask, as we knew that mother had no more money as we had already had a ride on those stupid donkeys. Suddenly I remembered! Nanny had given me sixpence that morning and it was still in the pocket of my coat. We ran to the van and asked for a cornet each – I can't remember tasting anything like it. We sat on the edge of the wall, licking our cornets, feeling very happy.

The numbers on the bus counted, we set off home. Just a few miles outside Aberystwyth, mother shouted, "Stop the bus! Gaynor is sick!" The bus eventually arrived at 'the top of the road' where my Dad was standing with Joy in his arms, waiting to hear about our day at the beach.

Thud

By Harry Lane

By the time they found him, it was far too late.

"Is he dead?"

"He's dead."

"Do you think it is him?"

"It's him".

The body had been washed up just below the weir. Wild sighed and looked around at the rain-leaden sky and the swollen river. The current was too strong to send the divers down.

"You're sure it's him?"

"I'm sure, Sir." Dwight looked at his Inspector.

"OK, I'll leave you here to carry on."

Wild pulled up his collar, turned and walked back along the tow path. He'd give it a little time then get in touch with the girl's mother and ask if she could bring her daughter down to the morgue to make a positive ID.

Four murders in four months: all blondes. He'd never been involved in anything like this before. The fifth month - the fifth girl. But she had managed to escape. There had been plenty of men watching the river when he'd struck, and this time they'd got him.

Time after time he'd told his wife not to go out unless it was absolutely necessary, and to stay well away from the tow paths... and to not even cut through the park.

It hurt him to look at his daughter. She was 16, blonde hair, blue eyes and peachy. Every time she went out he wondered if he would ever see her again. The whole town was in a grip of fear. Then the media had arrived and it had become a circus. The whole thing had become a bloody nightmare.

Thud.

Oosh! What's that noise? Where am I? It's so dark. I can hardly breathe. What happened?

Thud.

Oh, now I remember. That stupid girl: blonde, stuck up, flash blazer with a bag over her shoulder, short skirt and white socks. She and her friends always laughing, laughing at me as they passed, and me stood staring. They thought they were better than everyone else. But I'd marked her, been watching her for a while. Now, standing here among the bushes, waiting, I knew she'd be along. Not many people came near the river now, I'd made my mark, but she'd come. She'd come. Right on time, passing close. Out through the bushes, both hands around her throat, and back in again.

She'd got off a scream. Damn.

"Did you hear that?"

"Where?"

"Down by the bushes. Hurry".

Voices calling, some from upstream, others from the top of the bank near the main road.

The girl stepped back, twisted, and let fly, catching me on the left cheek just below the eye. She screamed again.

"Hurry."

Voices from above and along the path, this was bad.

"Aah!" She'd sunk her teeth into my hand, loosening my grip. She twisted once more and was gone, screaming, running through the bushes.

No time to waste. Out on to the path, looked right - there were two of them, plain clothed, coming hard. Another shout, and two more were running along the opposite bank. I turned and ran. I could hear them crashing through the undergrowth as they came down from the road above.

"He's heading your way!"

"Right."

Voices coming towards me from downstream. I sprinted faster.

"You're nearly on him. We'll stop him."

No way. They'll never get me. Just ahead was the small concrete jetty where they tied up the rowing boats. I'd grab one, take it out into midstream, sweep down past them, dump the boat and disappear into the town. They'd never get me.

Coming up just ahead: a leap, grab the iron rail, vault over, land. Damn. Twisted my ankle. Pitched forward, crashed, came down head first onto the concrete. Darkness, cold, sinking, drifting, just drifting.

Thud.

That noise again. What's going on? Hmm. There'd been four of them before this: all blonde, stuck up, and strutting their stuff. But I'd marked them. Waiting in the bushes until they'd passed: straight out, both hands around their neck, and back in. It was always the same: the muted scream, ramming my face into theirs, taking a lock of that blonde hair into my mouth and biting down hard as I increased the pressure on their throat. The flailing arms, the choked screams, twisting and turning, gagging, pleading, whinging and whining, and finally - that shuddered silence. I was exultant, victorious. This was good, this was great. I had triumphed again.

Then there was the Police. It never occurred to them that every time a body was washed up, I happened to be in the area, offering to lend a hand, even plunging fearlessly into the water to help free the victim from grasping roots, weeds and overhead branches. Then after the combined effort of getting the body up the bank, I'd helped carry them, gently, before lying them down on the soft grass. They never clicked, the Police, always thanking me for my assistance, and even commending me twice.

The funerals. I always went to the funerals, I wouldn't have missed them for the world. Pushing my way through the crowd, past the reporters and camera crews. Standing at the back of that packed church, listening to that stupid priest prattle on.

"He shall suffer, he who committed this heinous crime, when he comes to stand before his judgement day."

Rubbish, load of rubbish. Then outside, after the service, the mourners. I always mingled with the mourners. A handshake here, a pat on the back there, offering my condolences. Look at them. They're pathetic, hunched and drawn; afraid, definitely afraid.

Thud.

That bloody noise again. It woke me up. What is it? It feels like my head is exploding, I can't breathe, and this blackness - so thick and heavy, cloying.

Thud.

Not again. Do something. Pull yourself together. Come on, make a move. Arms, legs, my hands and feet - can't feel them. Can't feel anything.

Thud

What is it? I'm starting to panic now. I can smell my sweat falling off my face, running down my ribcage.

Thud.

Not so close, it's now more distant. For Heaven's sake, shout, scream, make a noise. I can't, my jaw doesn't work, my lips won't move.

Thud.

What is it? And then that searing jolt, and with it the realisation. Now I know.

Thud.

Softer and further away, almost soothing. Now I know what the noise is. It's the sound of soil falling and landing just above my face. Someone is shovelling earth, and I'm not yet dead.

The Dispensary

By Oonah V Joslin

Tatum walked through the deserted high suburbs towards the low white buildings of the Dispensary. The only residents here were the feral cats and vermin. Life on the outside was too harsh for her now so she had come for aid. She had skills, qualifications. Maybe not the skills they wanted but she would do anything.

Last time they'd given her nutritional supplements and turned her away. "This one is a super processor," she'd heard the chip analyst say, "Supplements only." That meant she wasn't from the genetic pool they wanted. She carried genes for obesity, intelligence and creativity. People like that had a tendency to be fat, physically lazy and imaginative enough to make trouble.

Tatum knew the buildings of the Dispensary well. She had helped develop the facility; had been instrumental in training some of the operatives. She had tried to give them a sense of moral responsibility for what they were doing. It was important that all the measures put in place to combat disease, provide employment and share resources be equitable and humane. Nowadays the operatives trained each other and left moral concerns to the Global Committee.

Tatum pulled the fur coat she'd found at the fill sites tight around her. She was more coat than woman now. Flurries of snow were beginning to fall. From this elevation she could still make out the coastline and the ever encroaching rubbish slick just off-shore. If the snow lay you wouldn't be able to see where the land ended and the great North Pacific Gyre began. It would all look like bleached plastic. They'd probably put her to work on that floating toxic heap. Still it didn't stink like... She looked back towards the land fills where she'd picked out a living. Life was rubbish whichever way she turned but at least this way she would stay alive.

The automatic door slid open. A mechanical voice said, "Welcome.

Please place your left wrist over the consul scanner." This had all been automated. She wondered what the chip analysts did for food these days. A barrier was lowered and she went into the booth.

"Chip expired," said the voice.

"What does that mean, 'chip expired'?" she asked, looking for the camera she knew was somewhere.

"Operator to booth 9."

A young man approached. "If you'd like to step this way um, Tatum," he said consulting an electopad.

"What does it mean expired?" Her voice wavered.

"The systems run off plasma processors now. They cannot interpret your chip. You will receive a new one."

"Right."

"Functions change. We will require fresh information."

Tatum looked at the bland and spartan surroundings. This kind of impersonal atmosphere was exactly what she'd fought to prevent. But efficiency and accountability had become expediency and dissenters to the new regime had been relocated. She wondered whether Dr. Fiche was still Director.

It was warm enough to remove her coat but she still shivered, missing its accustomed weight. In the booth there was a bed, a table and a chair. Tatum sat in front of the interactive screen and answered all the questions put to her, submitting with ill grace to the various scans.

"Age?"

"59..."

"Status?"

"Outsider. Super Processor."

"Last employ?"

Paneuropia Dispensary G666 C grade." It seemed a long ordeal. Each answer was verified by a RetNaScan.

"I will fit your chip," said the operative coolly.

"Will it hurt?"

He didn't answer. He swabbed her left wrist and removed the subdermal chip deftly. It hurt a little.

"Is there any work here? I'm a geneticist. I wrote, 'Mutant Man,' you know."

The operative made no reply.

"Dr. Tatum Fenton?"

Still there was no hint of recognition.

"Dr. Fiche would remember me."

The operative replaced the chip with one from the computer output tray. None of this technology was familiar to her and the young man, what was he? Some kind of robot?

"Can I get some food here? I'm so very hungry. I walked all the way down from the fills you see," she said. "It took me days." Her voice tailed off.

He remained impassive.

They brought her some real food if you could call it that. It looked grey and tasted synthetic. Afterwards she was asked to check the information on her new implant and confirm it with her secret pin number.

She waved her wrist over the scanner and the screen glowed green.

"There's nothing on here but today's date," she said.

"That is correct. Please insert your pin." The operative left.

Tatum keyed in the number. She felt the chip tingle in her arm and waited for the rest of the information to appear on the screen. Maybe it took a while to process. The young man had been so uncommunicative; she wasn't really sure what she was supposed to do. She was so tired though - drained - drained from years scavenging the fill sites, tired from the walk, exhausted and confused by all the new technology. At least it was warm here and she had a full stomach. Still the screen was blank and somewhat distorted. It was a relief to go and lie on the bed. She felt a little dizzy and heavy – as if she was falling...falling...

Set You Free

By Daniel Brown

"This is unacceptable" Val yelled. The Cat's ears twitched slightly at this outburst, but it otherwise remained unruffled, paying more attention to cleaning the pads between its back paws.

"It's just a door, for crying out loud. Open it." The Cat looked up at this sharp command, pupils wide and tail twitching.

"I'm Sorry. Please open the door." The Cat narrowed its eyes at Val, then resumed cleaning its back paw.

"Why am I even here?" The Cat looked up at Val once again, this time cool and appraising.

"Is it because of the accident? That wasn't my fault. She stepped out in front of me before I could even react. No one could have done anything differently." The Cat switched its attention to its front paws and began cleaning its ears with great ferocity.

"I've never been a bad person," Val said "I've always given to charity, never been cruel to anyone, why can't I go through?" The Cat glanced at Val, then switched ears.

"I've never been violent. Never stolen from anyone. I've always been honest with folk, told them the truth and all that."

The Cat looked up again, tail sweeping hard from side to side. Val *hadn't* ever struck anyone, or stolen anything. 'Always tell the truth', those were Val's watch words.

Slowly, at first, those truths came back to her.

"I wouldn't bother."

"It's not what I'd do."

"It's your own fault."

"That's not my problem."

"I don't care."

"You're wasting your time."

Val felt the strength seeping out of her legs. She looked around for somewhere to sit, but the featureless room was completely bare, save for herself, The Cat and... there was a door, somewhere, although she couldn't see it. The promise of egress hung in the air, although the method was unclear.

The Cat, satisfied for now, curled into a ball and began grooming its tail.

"I didn't mean to... It's not..." Val faltered, then clung to habit. "None of it was false." The Cat looked up, eyes now wide and ears flat to its skull. It rolled to its feet, tail extended behind, as rigid as a sword. The Cat was bigger than Val had first thought.

"You can't get wrong for speaking the truth." she told it.

Hissing and spitting, The Cat sprang forward and Val stumbled back with a whimper. The Cat was far, *far*, larger than she'd let herself see. Thinking The Cat was small, was like thinking Blenheim Palace was small because you could turn the doorknob with one hand. The stalking Cat filled her vision and Val fell to the bare floor with a sob as her own truth was revealed.

The honesty she'd always been so proud of was the biggest lie of them all. She'd always told the truth, but only when it was harsh and unnecessary. Pettiness and spite dressed up as 'No nonsense', meanness disguised as 'Speaking as I find' Her eyes screwed tightly closed, Val let out a low nasal moan and felt every moment of pain her so-called honesty had caused, all the hurt she'd inflicted by staying silent when the truth would have been pleasant or soothing to hear.

Time lost its meaning and Val let it go easily, replaced with pain and shame for who could know how long.

"I'm sorry." She whispered.

She heard a soft chirrup in reply and felt a tiny and rough tongue on her eyelids. When she opened her eyes The Cat was centimetres away from her face, its whiskers pointing forward and tail pointing straight up and curled at the tip like a question mark.

"Please can I go through?" The Cat purred and pushed its head into Val's chin. Her face still wet with tears, Val stood up and looked for the door she was sure should be there.

The Cat meowed and scurried behind her and Val felt, more than saw, a door opening somewhere in front of her. Her vision faded out for a second, as if she'd stepped into a dark room from bright sunshine.

When her sight cleared, Val found herself in a bare, featureless room. It was completely empty, save for herself, a small cat and a door... No, the *feeling* of a door somewhere. The Cat ignored her and began cleaning itself.

"No. This isn't fair. Why can't I pass through?" The cat paid her no mind.

"This is unacceptable." Val yelled. The Cat's ears twitched at this outburst but it otherwise remained unruffled, paying more attention to cleaning between the pads on its back paws.

The Smell of Success

By Kate Booth

The books for Liz to review were stacked on the left side of her desk. By the years of high speed reading and the experience of feeling the layout and quality of each book made her able to work fast. How the shine or rough fibres of quality paper and the binding of hardbacks made an impression on Liz's brain, she did not know. She always held each book in her hands and stroked the outside cover. If it smelt strongly enough to reach her nose, she let the aroma rise and fill her breath. If it gave off the acrid smell of formalin, this dampened Liz's whole impression of its text. Other books smelt of the wood they originated from, or even reflected the subject matter of the text. Cookery books were the worst for awakening her own senses and imagination. Surely her smelling smoky bacon or the yeasty aroma of freshly cooking bread or cakes must be a long lost memory, reminding her to eat.

The quality of paper set the stage for each author to spin their story out for their audience. Reviewing fictional stories was the major part of Liz's work load. Romances always 'felt' warm but only succeeded if the end was happy and satisfactory. They were so distinctive and quick to assess that Liz felt the urge to just write "More of the same". Murder mysteries were the vast majority of crime fiction she reviewed. They were often rather formulaic; so again, if Liz knew where the story was going; she felt disappointed if it lacked surprises or the plot was flat.

Today was *so* different. Her work had been laid out by the office manager, Bill Scott. Liz had run her eyes over the sleeves, surprised that all four editions were travel books. It was a subject close to her heart, as she was due a lot of holiday. The first had snapshots of European views and the dreaded word 'caravan' in the title. It reeked of formalin, and she could hear the screams and shouts of children letting off steam after hours of boring travelling in the back of cars. Childhood memories of feeling sick, and "When will we get there?" were hard to forget. Liz was sure that it would sell well, as an update version of changes to well visited and loved camping sites.

Next was the similar genre of 'Canal improvements in the UK' It would be added to years of similar but crumpled cabin books. She hoped that this one would include the recommended Pubs, or dates of festivals for people to aim for when walking away from the chugging engines of the canal. She picked it up and fanned the pages to get a sense of the planning. It felt just the same as the last few years, but it had a new section on the CAMRA 'Real' Ale awards. She looked forward to reading that, but maybe at the end of the day, before going home.

She waved her hand over all four books to review, and her eyes were drawn to the last book. A welcoming view of dramatic rising hills and the sinuous river complemented the title of the book - "Walking the Forests of Peru". Surrounding this view was a border of exotic colourful birds. As she reached out to pick up this volume she shrieked and yanked her hand back.

"God, that hurt!" she said as she nursed her hand.

Liz sat down in her chair, and leant forward to see if she had been electrocuted. Nothing was plugged in, so was it just static? She looked over her hand. No marks.

"Grow up Liz, You've just imagined it!" Talking to herself was not unusual, but her friend Stacey must have heard her cry of pain from her office next door.

"Are you OK Liz?" She listened patiently as Liz tried to explain her shocking experience. They checked for loose wires together, but were none the wiser. Stacey picked up the book without any problems and started to look over the beautiful cover.

"Wow, I would love to look over this book when you've finished your review, Liz." She held it out, but Liz stared at it hard, rather than taking it. Stacey put it down squarely on Liz's desk. "It's not going to bite you Liz, but you can't just forget about this book. Bob wants the first drafts by lunch time, 'cos he said they were only 'picture books.' Cheeky bastard, shout if you need me."

What a long hard think Liz had to have. She felt very unsettled. Where had her peace of mind gone? It felt like a big black cloud was heading her way, or heading for someone else; ready to rain and rain. But that happened like that, all over the world, all around the world, so where had this feeling of fear come from? She gingerly reached out both her hands and placed them squarely on the book. Her fear was still a tight knot of muscles in her stomach, but she would find the solution by moving on with her life.

Three weeks later Liz arrived at her local Starbucks and met Jake, the love of her life. She had set up a coffee for both of them, and was explaining her plan to join a charity, working out in Peru. They had welcomed her enquiries because the recent rains had caused a landslide which had buried a large area of unplanned housing.

Yes, she was going to have to work hard, for just enough pay to get her there, daily food and shelter. They had been very interested in her CV. The publishing contacts she was in touch with had passed on advice about recycling paper and plastics in Europe, and wanted her to research strategies for stabilising damaged earth works in hillside forests in of Peru.

Cattle rearing and intensive deforestation seemed to be a familiar cause of the land damage problem similar to those encountered in other parts of the world. What had startled Liz was that these strategies (i.e. cheap) hadn't been adopted by the small farmers in South American. She was going to look at previously successful solutions for preventing the dangers of landslides. She wasn't a farmer, or a logging expert, but she did know how to work with enthusiastic authors. People with ideas in print were usually very keen to be listened to.

Jack had sat in silence. He smiled and nodded to encourage his Liz to carry on her story. He had lots of questions and ideas of his own, but he knew that Liz had planned this talk, and interrupting her would throw her into a spin.

"Great job for a speed reader, Liz." He gathered her up in his arms and gave her a big kiss.

"Do you think there would be room for an enthusiastic 'soul mate', who wants to travel with you?" he said. "I still want to see the world, and I will die of boredom if I have to make any more coffee and profit for Starbucks. Oh and by the way, have we got time to get married? Before that flight that they want me to catch as well? I'm sorry that I have been so slow; but you showed me that lots of enthusiasm can move your life forward. I want to share your life, Liz, and find a way to share your intuition. Your new skills at foretelling the future are an amazing gift and I want to go on loving and supporting you. OK?"

Liz nodded. She knew this was coming….some time.

A Quote and 100 Words (mine took 117)

By Margaret Kerswell

There was a dream. There was my life. There was my death. I woke up, and it was real…

It was dark when I opened my eyes, I felt disorientated, crushed, I couldn't explain why. I tried to sit as the need to urinate washed over me. My head hit a hard surface and landed back on my pillow, "What on earth?" I muttered, I reached to rub my head, I couldn't do it, my hand struck the same surface, a few inches above.

Panic set in, I felt around with my hands, walls on either side of me and a realisation, it hadn't all been a dream, it was real, I'd been buried! Then I screamed…

Earth, Wind, Fire and Water

By Martin Booth

In a small French village, somewhere in the mountains, four figures sat around a table outside a café. They had been there for a while and the table already held an empty carafe of the local red wine and four glasses. One of the figures, a woman in a flowing dress of reds and oranges and yellows, waved a hand and the waiter brought another carafe, which he set down and removed the empty one. The woman held it up to the light. "Poor vintage this year…"

"I fear for the industry," said the man. He was dressed in browns and greens and greys. At first his clothes looked like combat fatigues, but they were too indistinct for that. "Too much heat withers the grapes on the vines."

Fire looked sharply at Earth. "Are you blaming me for this?" she asked, holding up the wine. "What about a lack of water to irrigate the crops properly?"

The third member of the group adjusted her sunglasses. She wore a long, flowing blue dress which seemed to fall and skip across the contours of her body. "I do my best," she said, "but it's very hard when you're trying to do something and you're ripped from the ground and thrown into the air far too violently!"

Air chuckled and poured herself a glass. "Oh, but ma Cherie, I thought you liked that..?" She sipped the wine and grimaced. "But you are right. Things are getting, er, out of hand." She put the glass back down, her dress almost floating around her, its colours difficult to describe, changing from white to blue to black to covered with tiny gleaming stars.

Earth tapped lightly on the table. "Come on, ladies, we have a job to do. Let us start our meeting and see what happens."

Water almost lay back in her seat. "It's always the same," she muttered. "We look at what we've done in the past decade, then what we need to do and then go our separate ways. Je m'ennuie."

"Be that as it may," said Earth, "but things are getting out of hand, and very quickly, too. I think that in ten years' time it may be too difficult to put right."

Fire, who had been sitting lighting her fingertips and then blowing them out, emptied her wineglass. "Then perhaps we should start again, yes?"

Silence descended on the group, then Water spoke. "Did I hear you right?"

"Yes, darling. Clear away the brushwood and start again."

"It all sounds very dramatic… very Biblical," said Water. "What about all the people?"

Fire clicked her fingers, sending sparks onto the table. "Paf!"

"Anyway," said Air, "we're strictly non-denominational… no apocalypses."

It was down to Earth to lead the discussion forward. "As Elementals, we are above all that. But, I agree, we do need to do something."

"Politics?" suggested Water, diluting her wine to make it slightly more palatable.

"Too… ephemeral," said Air, her dress floating in the hot breeze. "After all, we've been here for billions of years."

"Those were the days!" said Fire. "Volcanoes and asteroids and lava… magnificent!"

Earth tapped on the table again. "Yes… but we are much more even now, much more in balance."

"And there's the problem," retorted Fire. "We're not in balance. I suggest we simply do nothing!"

Air stopped fidgeting and the heat of the day became still and oppressive. "Nothing?"

"No. Let the environment sort itself out." Fire ignited the menu card while she thought. "Shouldn't take more than, well, until our next meeting. Let the sea levels rise…"

"Actually, I quite like that idea," chipped in Water.

"Can I remind you that you've already got almost three quarters of this planet anyway," began Earth. "And you keep pinching bits of mine."

Air moved to lean forwards and the breeze began to shift the heat around. "Enough, enough! We are Elementals. We are above all this. It's not our fault that the humans have messed up the balance. All we do is look after the base forces. If bad stuff happens, we try to sort it out, but we don't actually control stuff to that degree."

"So what are you suggesting we do?" said Fire. "Intervene or not?"

Before she could answer, Water held up her hand. "I've got a suggestion."

The others looked at her. "Why don't we simply find another world to look after? One that's not so messed up as this one is becoming. I mean, there must be millions of other planets out there!"

"Indeed there are," said Earth, "and it's a reasonable idea. However, have you stopped to think that each world might just have its own Elementals?"

Water looked crestfallen. "So we're sort of… stuck here?" she said.

"'Fraid so."

She looked around. "We have been a little lax over this, haven't we?" she said, finally.

The others nodded. "So what do we do?" asked Air.

"Make a plan, I guess," said Earth. "What have we got to sort out?"

It was Water who started. "Well, my resources are being evaporated too quickly and from places they're needed," she said. "Il **fait trop chaud**. I need it to be cooler."

"I'm sorry, darling, I don't have a choice," said Fire. "The atmosphere is changed, keeping in too much of my heat. I can't get rid of it."

They both looked at Air. "Not my fault, people. I'm being slowly poisoned by the stuff from the ground. I do my best, but sometimes I can't keep in all that water and I'm afraid I drop it where it shouldn't be!"

Earth sighed. "So it's my earth that's causing this, is it? Can I remind you about being washed away by too much water or burned up by too much Fire?"

An argument was about to break out when the waiter brought another carafe of wine. Fire looked at it, and waved it away. The waiter shrugged and went back to the relative cool of the kitchen. Finally, Air sent a puff of wind to rapidly chill the others. They stopped and looked at her. "It seems as though we have a circular argument here," she said. "We're all part of the problem so we all need to be part of the solution."

"What do we do then?" asked Earth.

"That," said Air, "is what we have to decide…"

About time!

By Oonah V Joslin

"What now?" asked Phil.

"Wait I suppose." Geraldine sat down. She was out of puff and not getting any younger.

"If anyone can get to the bottom of this Roger can," said Phil.

"Here's Roger now," Martha said.

"What is it?" asked Roger.

"It's a hole," said Martha.

"Archaeology?" asked Roger. "Any remains?"

"That's just it," said Peter, "there appears to be nothing."

"Nothing?"

"Nothing *at all*."

"I hope you're not wasting my time here," said Roger. "I'm supposed to be supervisory and I have a life you know. How far down did you go down?"

"Six feet," said Martha. "We were only trying to get a sideways shaft into the barrow you see. We didn't need to get down far to do that. And because I'm the slimmest I thought I might worm my way through. Then it all just slipped and"

"We barely got her out," continued Peter.

"I was just dangling over nothing," said Martha.

"Took all four of us pulling," said Geraldine.

"and my head was spinning!" said Martha. "It was almost like something was *dragging* me in."

"Suction mud?"

"No mud," said Martha. "Look I'm clean as a whistle."

"Sink hole then."

Peter beckoned Roger over and shone a torch into the hole.

"Well that's the darnedest..." said Roger. "It looks just matt black but with dizzying depth."

"Thought it might be the entrance to a series of potholes or caves." suggested Phil.

"Here, give me that torch. You'd think you'd see the light going farther down," Roger observed. "It's like the light's being swallowed. Well there's only one way to find out what's down there or what kind of phenomenon this is. Glad I brought some sturdy equipment. I don't suppose there's any anchorage hereabout?"

It was all scrub and moorland; featureless but for the large earth mound directly behind the hole."

"Us?" volunteered Phil.

"Well okay... Better not let me down now," said Roger.

"Look, I'm experienced," said Peter. "I could come with you – for safety."

"Well I thought at first a preliminary investigation – quick look. Maybe just lower me down with a light; see what we're up against, pull me back up when I shout. If this is a major excavation, I'll have to come back with a team anyway Peter but thanks for the offer."

"Okay. Good." Peter was kind of relieved.

Roger suited up and as they lowered him over the edge, they found themselves staring into a black vortex. Time passed.

"What now?" asked Phil.

"Wait I suppose."

"If anyone can get to the bottom of this Roger can."

"Here's Roger now."

"What is it?"

"It's a hole."

Toward the Light

By Harry Lane

Toward the light. How often had I heard that? 'Go Toward The Light', that peaceful, restful last journey. With head up, no fear in your heart, just serene confidence as you step over into the other side.

It was Christmas Eve - not that that made me smile: I never smiled. The car was parked up at the edge of the sand dunes, the beach stretched out below and then the beckoning sea. As usual we were staying at Uncle's... the family, me – the thirty eight year old spinster who made everyone despair and who had given up on herself. The same old routine. I wanted a bit of space, so any excuse and I drove here to sit in silence and brood, looking back on the pages of my life that had never been turned.

At School I wasn't bullied, really, more ignored. It was as though I wasn't there... school trip to Blackpool somebody flicked Candy Floss into my hair. Wearing Nanna's green cardigan on a cold day didn't even raise a laugh. Running home, fast over the fields and getting stuck in the mud having to take off socks and shoes and carry on barefoot while everyone looked on, typical. Drifting from one dull job to the next after I left school. Then the final humiliation: a fortnight before my wedding my intended went off with a so-called best friend. So on and on and on.

Tonight I was going to change all that. I was resigned, or so I thought. That phrase 'Toward The Light' had always captivated me, now more than ever. I think I'm ready to put it to the test. Leaving the car I walk down to the beach, a biting wind coming in from the sea, swirls of sand spiralling upwards and disappearing into the dark, clear night. Wave caps frosted by a haloed moon. Along the beach, collar turned up, hair ruffled, my stride a little hesitant. Ahead a rock point spearing out from the dark right angle of the cliffs, breakers pounding and crashing on its tip, surging up the flat rocks before being sucked back abruptly into that boiling, constantly moving vortex.

I stumble as I start to mount the rocks... they're not very high but my foot is uncertain. Cliff at my back I gaze down the point to the sea... can't make out much just a swirling blackness topped with ice flecks. So my journey begins, one which has been coming inevitably to this time and this place. I take my first step. The rocks are smooth and undulating, heading straight out to the point, the surf rolling up and then being snatched back into the maelstrom. My progress was steady after the rocks began to feel slippery, my feet and legs getting soaked with spray. A few steps further the foam was around my knees and I staggered as it returned to the sea. Suddenly the rock dropped sharply and the oncoming wave lifted me off my feet, taking me further up the rocks and then literally dragging me back on its return. I was amazed at the speed and power, and totally unprepared.

All of a sudden there was nothing beneath my feet, I was surrounded by foam and enveloped in a clinging chill. I thrashed automatically but seemed to get dragged out and down, the water boiling over my head and before my eyes. Next a huge surge and I was thrown back and I could feel the rocks bumping and scraping as I tumbled over them. I had to do something – this was not how it was meant to be... There was no peace, nothing tranquil here. This wasn't a step: I was being dragged, tossed back and forth like a rag doll. I tried to put my feet down, regain my balance and stand up straight. But to no avail as the wave returned: I was picked up and carried straight into the sea

Now I was scared, this time I seemed to be taken further out and dragged down deeper, the cold and blackness more intense. My heart was pounding in my ears, my mouth was clamped shut, the noise roaring and thudding above, my head about to explode and somewhere in the distance two red pinpricks of light. This couldn't be it... not like this.

Once again the sea coughed forth and I was flung forward, my head breaking the surface, my arms and legs thrashing as though by themselves as I was hurtled towards the point. Desperately trying to get a footing but not this time, the wave carrying me over the rocks. I could feel nothing beneath me and hearing a great roar filled with malice and mocking the wave returned me to the sea. Turning my head I saw behind me, black and towering, a wall of water. Deposited at the foot of it I looked up... dark, faceless, expressionless, yet rippling as though flexing its muscles for the onslaught. High above where the wave crested the roar kissed the spray and the white sea-mares played, leaping, prancing, kicking, galloping in the foam.

For a moment time seemed to slow, then they saw me and reared up. Their keening heard high above the wind. Manes flowing, nostrils flaring they started to bear down on me, hooves striking out, backs arched and tails streaming out behind. With the curve of the wave they came, eyes rolling, lips drawn back tight exposing their teeth in a wicked smile, ears flat against their skulls, straining, reaching, arching down the wall of water like tortured dancers in a macabre ballet. And then they struck...

A last fractured gasp of air then I went under spinning round, no longer sure where the surface was. My heart was hammering, my lungs gripped by a steel band and my throat and mouth aching. I felt as though I was being squeezed smaller and smaller and this time the pinpricks of light were behind my eyes. Whether I kicked and struggled I'm not sure but all of a sudden the wind hit me lifting me half out of the water and the cold air slammed into my lungs like an ice-tipped javelin. High above the keening of the white mares and the roar of the sea I heard something else, something high and brittle and gut-wrenchingly real, a scream... it was me screaming.

At that moment came the light. I saw the light, a white light. "She's here, she's here, she's here!" And then I roared, I roared for being nothing at school, for not getting noticed, staying in the background and saying nothing. I roared for every dead-end job, for every failed relationship, for the pity sent my way and for the apathy felt. I roared for Nanny's green cardigan, for Candy Floss in my hair. I roared once more to run, barefoot down the lane. I roared. Then the light again, close, closer… white lights, torchlight back and forth, shifting left and right glaring through the night, arching over the waves. "We have her, we have her!"

I smile, I have ended where I began, going toward the light.

The Altar of Bones

By Margaret Kerswell

The altar of bones stood in the corner and made Jaime's blood run cold. She was not usually freaked out by this kind of thing; over the years she'd seen more than one, but this, this was different.

All the other altars Jaime had seen were made from animal bones One of the most impressive ones had been made with bovine skeletons and decorated with sheep and goat skulls.

This however was constructed from human bones. It was decorated with human skulls in a variety of sizes from child's to adults.

Slowly Jaime crossed the dimly lit room to take a closer look……..as well as the skulls which adorned the top of the altar, there were some skulls which had been converted to chalices (for want of a better word). These chalices had lids which had been fashioned from the tops of the crania themselves.

Jaime fought the urge to be sick as she lifted the lid from one of the smaller skulls. She took a tentative look inside and was greeted with the sight of a blood and eyeball concoction. Quickly replacing the lid she headed back outside to pull herself together, not before emptying her stomach contents at the side of the street however.

'What kind of sicko has done this?' she thought.

Jack Who Had Two Faces

By Daniel Brown

As these words were given to me, so I give them to you, freely and without obligation. All know of Jack Who Killed the Giant, and many have heard of Jack Who Was His Father, but few the tale of Jack Who Had Two Faces...

Though his father was a chieftain of great renown, his name is now forgotten to all but the wisest and oldest, of which I am neither. Jack however, had never forgotten it, nor the names of his brothers and bondsmen, whom the men on the great horses took. Like a storm they had fallen upon the forts and villages of Jack's people, sudden and unrelenting. His people had fallen and their heads were taken to decorate the strangers' saddles. Jack had lived, for his spear was sharp and his lungs larger than any but the greatest giant, but without the heads of his people, he had fled for naught. His victories in single combat, his ambushes and narrow escapes meant nothing to him or to those who would judge his deeds in the Otherworld.

Jack had wandered the woods, he had gone to the Groves and the ponds, given gifts to the waters and begged of the gods to give him aid, but none heard, or else none replied. Perhaps the strangers' Gods stole his words, who can say? In grief and despair, he travelled to the darkest heart of the Great Wood to offer his head to the ones who live beneath for aid in his revenge. Some say that he met them there that day and sealed his bargain, still others say that could not be so, since the gifts of the ones below always corrupt and taint the thing they were given to aid. I tell you now what was told to me, mayhap wiser heads then mine can decide who gave Jack his gift...

Walking into the dark heart of the Great Wood, Jack saw upon the path a young woman. Fair to look upon and enticing in her manner, she called out to Jack.

"Stay a while," she implored him. "Great warriors pass this way but rarely, and I would have a strong father for my sons." So, saying, she raised her skirts and made to lie upon the forest floor.

"Hold, woman!" Jack told her. "Will your sons aid me in my revenge?" The woman looked upon Jack's face and saw there no hint of lust or desire.

"In time, perhaps. But sons need a strong father, to become great warriors," she said. "Stay a while and you can raise an army to take your revenge."

"A man's revenge is not to be taken by his sons," he told her. "A grey beard who shrinks from battle all his life to send out his sons to do his work deserves no victory." And so saying, he passed her by.

Many days and nights passed as Jack travelled on and many beasts of the forest tried to make Jack their meal, but his spear was as swift as ever and footsore and weary, he found himself glad of the sight of a camp fire on the path ahead. Upon approaching the fire, he saw a trader and his bag of goods resting there.

"Greetings warrior!" said the trader. "Many weeks have I wandered in this forest, accosted by beasts both known and fey. For your company to the Great Wood's edge, I would pay you enough gold to make a statue of your own likeness."

"If you are willing to travel with me for a while," said Jack, "I shall gladly escort you out once my errand here is run."

"This is too slow!" the trader cried. "Perhaps if I gave you the gold I spoke of, and also enough iron to make swords for a hundred men, would you accompany me to the forest's edge?" Looking upon Jack's face, the merchant saw no sign of greed or avarice.

"Would your gold aid me in my revenge?" Jack asked him.

"Why, with enough gold you could hire so many warriors as to fill a wheat field from edge to edge."

"What use are ten thousand warriors," asked Jack, "to a man who is too weak to fight his battles for himself? A man should rely only on his kin and bondsmen in matters of honour," and so saying, he left the fire and slept elsewhere that night.

For many more days he travelled inwards, avoiding the tramplings of enormous creatures too terrifying to look upon, scurrying from tree root to hollowing, no different from a mouse who senses the owl's passing. After days of terror and nights passed in watchful tension, Jack was surprised to come upon a Bard, travelling towards the Heart also.

"Hail warrior!" the Bard said, "I feel in need of a rest, but am loath to do so alone in such a strange place as this, would you stay awhile and tell me your tale? I feel the urge to make a new song and the deeds of a man such as yourself must surely be worthy of renown."

"Would renown aid me in my revenge?" Jack asked him.

"Why, with a great song about your deeds, men would tremble at your very name," the Bard said. "Your enemies would be ready to give up before any battle was joined!"

"What use is it if my enemies fear the name they hear in songs?" Jack asked. "A man's enemies should tremble at the sight of him, not the memory of tales told around the fireside." With that, Jack strode ahead and left the Bard far behind him.

The moon grew and shrank twice, as Jack travelled further into the Heart of the Great Woods, but no closer did he seem to the place where the world below met ours. After many weeks alone, Jack's heart was gladdened to see another person on the path, an old woman travelling in the direction Jack had just come from, her back bent beneath a great bundle of sticks suitable for making charcoal.

"Greetings young warrior!" she said. "Would you aid an old woman with her burden?"

"Will your burden aid me in my revenge?" Jack asked her.

"What sort of a question is that?" the crone said. "Are you planning on stealing my sticks?" Jack's laughter roared out, shaking the treetops and startling the few birds that remained this far into the Great Wood out of the canopy. Jack took the crone's burden onto his shoulders and began to walk in the direction the crone had been walking.

"Hold a moment, warrior!" she told him. "Are you sure you wish to aid me? My hut lies at the very edge of the Great Wood, many weeks journey away from where you were heading."

"What use is revenge to a man who has forgotten how to be a man?" he asked her. "No matter how a man's heart burns for its desire, he shouldn't forget to be of use." The old woman nodded in approval.

"This is so. Follow me warrior, the way is long and the forest gives nothing away freely." With that she strode off at speed and Jack struggled to keep up with her, as the weight of the crone's burden bent his back and strained his knees.

Long they travelled, and many were the beasts that set upon them, which Jack defeated, and many also were the times they lost the path in the night, which Jack always found again. Always they pressed onwards and in time, they came to the crone's hut at the very line where the Great Wood gave way to the lands of men.

"Set aside your burden," the crone told Jack, "the time has come for us to part ways." Jack set down the sticks, glad to be free of the weight that had borne him down for so long. "Tell me warrior, what is your name?"

Jack thought hard for a moment, it is said that knowing the name of a person or thing gives one power over them. Jack thought about giving her his earned name of Giant Slayer, but in the end, he told her his true name.

"A fine name it is," she said, "Know this Jack, you shall have your revenge, but it shall earn you no glory to pass on to your sons, no plunder and no honour, for none shall know of your victory until long after our people have faded into the mists and all memory of us is buried beneath those who lie across the sea. Will you have it?"

"I will," he answered. The old woman nodded, and having made his choice she leaned into Jack and began to whisper into his ear. She told him of the way to see into men's hearts as surely as he saw into his own, the way to wear the faces of those long dead and the secret pathways that would take him all across the land in secret and at great speed.

Armed with his new knowledge, Jack crossed the land from north to south and east to west listening for the sound of heavy horses and after many weeks of searching, he heard the sound of the great horses the strangers rode upon. Jack's blood sang for vengeance, but he remembered the deaths of his kinsmen and bondsmen, who were not warriors of false renown and knew that he could not kill the whole band of his enemies alone. Instead, he listened to the hearts of those strangers closest to him and heard their fears for what would happen to them for keeping the heads of their enemies, for such was the custom of Jack's people, not the custom of the strangers, and one they undertook only to show the people of the land their power. Jack thought on this, as he waited for nightfall.

After night fell and the moon had almost finished the journey across the sky, Jack listened again to the hearts of the strangers and felt their fear grow stronger as the darkness closed in and the fires burned low. He heard the memory of the now dead great shaman who had so harshly warned against the taking of trophies from the bodies of the dead.

Jack was taken then with a notion, which he followed on immediately. Wearing the face of the great shaman the strangers remembered, he stole into their camp and threw a rock he had picked up for just that purpose onto the fire, sending sparks flying into the black night.

"Dishonour!" he yelled at the top of his powerful voice. "Dishonour and infamy! You who heard my words and did not heed them are damned and your souls and those of your families are cursed until the great spiral turns again! No peace shall you know in this world or the Other. Shadows shall follow you always, snapping at your heels and feasting on your essence until you are but shades yourselves, doomed to roam the world in darkness and shadow, hiding in dark corners from the light. Discard the heads you stole, then fall upon your swords, or else your line shall be cursed backwards and forwards for one hundred generations!" Quickly, Jack emptied a flask of strong spirit on the fire and as the strangers yelled in panic and fear at the gout of blue flame that erupted, he slipped from their camp, smiling at the sounds of heads landing outside the camp where they had been flung hastily and the dying screams of men falling upon sharp blades.

Having gathered up the returned heads and sung the songs of rest before taking once again to the secret roads, Jack followed the Strangers as they rode on. He heard the fear in the hearts of those who had not fallen on their blades, the doubts of those who suspected trickery from The People and many other secrets, both light and dark and deeply buried. As the sky began to darken, Jack once again thought on what he would do that night.

Jack stole up to the edge of the Stranger's camp and was surprised to see how many of them had fallen upon their swords, so many that there were almost few enough for him to fight them directly, but he resisted the song of vengeance racing through his blood. Dead men take no revenge in this world and Jack was loathe to wait until he entered Otherworld for his.

Once more wearing the face of the great shaman, Jack sneaked into the camp. He carried no rock this time, nor any strong spirit for the fires. As the strangers sat down for their meal of pottage and rabbit, he simply took a seat among those who were left. So intent were the Strangers on their food that no-one noticed him taking his ease, assuming that their scouts would prevent anyone from entering the camp unnoticed. He smiled to himself and decided that now was the time for him to speak.

"Enjoy your meal, blood sinners. The Otherworld holds no such pleasures for tainted souls." The faces of the remaining Strangers were a joy in Jack's heart, as he saw the ashen grimaces and abject fear written into them. The braver souls amongst them fumbled for their weapons, but the movements were half-hearted and Jack knew none would attack him. "Those of you who have refused to atone for your sin may still yet do so, but none who live past this night. I shall return after sunset tomorrow, for those who still cling to this world thinking it may give them safety." With that he stood up and walked calmly from the camp, once again hearing the thump of discarded heads and a few more death screams.

As he strode past terrified scouts and entered the secret pathways once out of their sight, he heard the Stranger's leader bellowing for his men to be strong and not fall prey to the trickery of weak foreigners. He listened to the hearts of those who were left and knew it was only the strength of their leader that held them from breaking and running. He knew in his own heart that tomorrow night, he must approach the camp with the Stranger's leader out of his tent and waiting for Jack's arrival. Under cover of full darkness, Jack gathered up the heads of his fallen people and sang the songs of rest, then prepared his weapons and his body, knowing that tomorrow his blood would have the vengeance it sang for.

All the next day he followed the Strangers, listening to the apprehension growing in their hearts and to the anger growing in the heart of their leader as they now numbered so few that Jack could pick out the individual hearts that he listened to. He longed to be amongst them, his spear dancing left and right, opening the throats and bellies of those who had dishonoured his people, but he had spoken of coming to them at nightfall and would not shame the day of his vengeance by breaking his word.

As the Strangers began to make camp for the night, Jack waited for the sunset by singing the songs of The People and promising vengeance to the shades of those still dishonoured by their heads being kept as trophies by those not of The People. With the setting of the sun, he wore once again the face of the great shaman and took up his weapons and walked boldly into the Stranger's camp.

This time, the Strangers were waiting for him, many with their weapons drawn, although he could see with his own eyes the looks of fear on the faces and the trembling of the hands holding swords or spears. He listened to the hearts of those surrounding him, and knew that their leader was waiting in his tent for the sound of Jack's voice so that he would know when to come out amongst the men and try to allay their fears. Jack gave thought to trying again to encourage some of them to fall on their blades, but decided that those who hadn't done so already wouldn't do so now. Without a word being spoken, he lashed out with his spear, felling the three men nearest to him before the Strangers had time to realise that Death was amongst them.

At the sound of battle being joined, their leader stormed out of his tent with weapons ready. Even that great warrior blanched at the sight of the great shaman from his youth, now cold many years past, slaughtering his best fighters with the skill and ease of a tempered warrior. Letting loose a cry to shake the mountains, the leader of the Strangers rushed into the fight. Even Jack was startled by the ferocity of the great Stranger's onslaught and he fell back briefly, blood gouting from a wound on his arm where the Stranger's sword had grazed him.

"False Shadow!" he bellowed. "What spirit bleeds when cut? What demon fights with the weapons of men?" He looked around the handful of men he had left alive. "This impostor unmanned our brethren? This is what terrified you all? Strengthen your arms and slay the deceiver!"

Jack knew then that his ruse was finished. He smiled at the Strangers and let them see his true face for the first time. The change seemed to unsettle some of the Strangers even further, which pleased him.

"Look upon the face of your Deathbringer. See the man who will send you all into the Otherworld for the dishonour you brought upon The People. Sing your Deathsongs, for none of you shall see the sunrise again." Jack told them. Some of the Strangers looked shaken and began chanting to themselves. Their leader roared at them to be silent.

"Stay your craven mouths! No more of us shall die this night, this coward who wears two faces will die here, by your hands or mine he shall die." With that the great Stranger once more unleashed his war cry and charged at Jack. Jack kept his silence, making no war cry of his own. This battle wasn't for the Gods to watch, but for The People, and those to whom it mattered would already be watching.

The clash of weapons and screams of those wounded and killed carried on long into the night, for the Great Stranger was no warrior of mean or ordinary skill and every time Jack aimed a killing blow at one of the lesser warriors, the Great Stranger would turn it aside, or aim a killing blow of his own which Jack had to avoid. As the light from the great fire the Strangers had built faded to a glow, Jack killed the last of the mean warriors so that only he and the Great Stranger remained alive. Both men pulled back slightly, to gain a moment to breath before the final clash which would end in death for one of them.

"Tell me your name, warrior." The Great Stranger said. "No great warrior should go to the ground unknown to his enemy."

"I am Jack, called Giant Slayer by The People and called Jack Who Was His Father, by the Horse People." The Great Stranger nodded in approval.

"Even in our lands, your stories are told. Great will be the honour I bring my Kinsfolk when I tell them how I bested the Giant Slayer, Jack Who Was His Father, Jack Who Wore Two Faces." Jack looked up then, for the first time in many long and bloody hours, and saw the glow that signals the coming of the sun. He remembered his promise earlier that night that none would see the sunrise. He reached behind himself and with all of the speed and strength that he had left, he withdrew the small knife he kept there for skinning animals and cutting ropes and flung it at the Great Stranger. The knife landed in the Great stranger's arm causing him to drop his sword. Jack leapt forward and plunged his spear into his enemy's chest. As the Great Stranger fell to the ground, he looked up at Jack with fury in his eyes. "What coward's behaviour is this?" he asked. Jack looked down on the man who had brought shame and dishonour on his people.

"The only dishonour in revenge is failing to take it once it has been declared." The Great Stranger began to chant his Deathsong, but Jack knew that a warrior of the prowess of the Great Stranger would not have a short list of deeds to recount. He pulled his knife from his dying enemy's arm. "I swore that none of you shall see the sunrise again and time grows short, but I will grant you your Deathsong, which is greater honour than you showed my people." With that said, Jack gouged out the Great Stranger's eyes so that he would keep his bond, while still honouring his enemy's Deathsong.

After his enemy died, Jack gathered up the last of the stolen heads of The People and sang the Songs of Rest. With the honour of The People satisfied, Jack turned in the direction of the Great Wood, thinking of a woman there who wished for sons and perhaps, in time, a clan of strong young men and women of The People.

I like the dead

By Martin Booth

"I like the dead. They make good conversation."

The man sitting opposite me looked up from his notebook with a quizzical expression on his face. I thought it was a perfectly normal thing to say, but apparently not. "You mean you enjoy talking about dead people... people who have died," he said.

"No. Real, actual dead people. They make really good conversation."

The man – I assumed he was a psychiatrist – put his head slightly on one side. "And why is that, Peter? What do they say to you?"

Before I answered I looked around the white painted room, with its one table, two chairs and the locked steel door. I knew that on the other side was a nurse, or warder, or prison officer, call them what you will. I had been sitting in the graveyard, having a perfectly civil conversation with a couple I'd got to know when someone had wondered what I was doing and called the police.

I went back to the task in hand. "Think about it for the minute," I said. "In any churchyard there are people from all ages of history, sometimes going back to the Middle Ages. The stuff they can tell me, just about everyday life, is fascinating."

The psychiatrist furrowed his brows. "But, Peter, they're dead. They can't talk to anyone."

"Oh but they can," I replied. "The thing you're forgetting is that they've all done the death thing." I leaned forwards, and the psychiatrist leaned back slightly. "They have died and seen what's on the other side. They know!"

"And have they told you?" The psychiatrist made a few notes. "Have they told you what is... on the 'other side'?"

I shook my head. "Well, no, it seems they're not allowed to... you know, all the God and Heaven stuff. But from what I've seen and heard, it looks as though the afterlife is pretty much like the 'fore'life, if you see what I mean?"

"Not really." I could tell that the shrink was getting bored... Here I was, some nutter picked out of a churchyard at midnight sitting on a tombstone supposedly talking to the dead. But really, it was true. I could talk to the dead. The shrink tried another tack. "So, er, how long have you been able to do this?" he asked in a neutral tone of voice.

I thought back to when I realised what I could do. "Since about the age of eight... well, that's when I realised what I could do," I said. "Before that I just spoke to those nice people who spoke to me. I was just being polite, like my parents told me to be. I didn't realise that they weren't living."

More scribbles on the page. For all I knew he could have been drawing cartoons to keep himself amused, because he made sure I couldn't see the page. "So when did you realise? It must have been quite a shock, yes?"

"No."

He began to look really puzzled now. "But you were, what..?" He consulted his copious cartoons: it couldn't have been a minute since I'd told him. Jeez! Talk about someone just going through the motions to collect his pay. However, unless I thought about this very carefully, that's exactly what I'd be going through – the motions – and I mean that in its scatological context.

"Eight. It was when my Uncle Arnold died. I went to the funeral and everyone was really sad, but I wasn't because I could see him sitting on top of the coffin. Just before it was lowered into the flames he hopped off and sat at the back of the chapel. Big smile on his face, too!"

The psychiatrist stopped his scribbling and looked at me. "And why do you think he was smiling?" he asked.

"I asked him later on," I said. "Remember, I was only eight years old. He said that he finally felt free. I didn't understand what he meant, but later on I found out that he had a really miserable marriage, so I guess he had managed to get out, finally."

"But were you never frightened?" he asked. "I mean, all these dead people around. That's not normal, is it?"

I looked him straight in the eye. "It is to me."

There was a silence in the room as the psychiatrist made yet more notes, looked at me, stared at the barred window and chewed the end of his pen. For my part, I sat and just looked at my hands and listened to the muted sounds of the hospital through the strong door. Finally, the psychiatrist took in a deep breath. "I have been thinking hard about your case," he said. "Liar," I thought. "However, I would like to do some more studies," he said with the gravitas of someone who could leave the room whenever he wants. "If that is alright?"

If it gets me out of here, I thought, fine. "What, exactly, do you have in mind, doc?" I asked. "As long as it doesn't involve surgery!"

He smiled, a purely professional smile. "Of course not." Again, liar. "We need to do scans of you while you are having one of your episodes. I mean, can you actually see these dead people at will?"

"Not really. I can choose to ignore them, if I'm busy, much the same as you can ignore ordinary living people. But I can't control them in any way. I can't suddenly make a dead person appear and do my bidding. If you think that's the case you've been watching too many movies on the Syfy channel."

The psychiatrist scratched his head. He wasn't making much of an inroad this morning and it was beginning to annoy him. I wasn't trying to, but when someone is being so much of a dick you just can't help it. I was about to launch into another speech about confusing my gift with black arts or sorcery when I became aware of a dead person wandering into the room. I looked across the room, behind the psychiatrist's shoulder and saw my Uncle Arnold wander into the room. He looked well and happy and waved to me across the room.

"Hiya, young 'un. Everything all right?"

"Not quite, Uncle."

The psychiatrist's head jerked up. "Who are you talking to?" he demanded.

I smiled. "Oh, it's my Uncle Arnold – you know, the one I told you about. He's popped in to see how I am."

The psychiatrist spun round in his chair and looked at the room. To him, it appeared completely empty apart from us and the table and chairs. "Where is this... spirit?" he asked in a tight voice.

"Spirit!" said Uncle Arnold. "Who is this Victorian? Shall I go to the spirit store and buy some ectoplasm to chuck over him?"

"If you like," I said. "Probably do him good. Tell you what, Uncle. Can you go and stand in that corner. I want to do an experiment."

"Excuse me," said the psychiatrist, "I will do the experiments."

"Humour me." I got up and waved for the psychiatrist to do the same. I pointed him towards the corner in which Uncle Arnold was standing patiently. "Right," I said, "Go into that corned and see if you can feel or see anything." Even I wasn't sure what would happen, but it was worth a try. The psychiatrist walked towards the corner, then he stopped and peered forward very hard. Then he walked forward a bit further and finally stood in the corner. "What am I supposed to…" he started then stopped. Through the psychiatrist's chest I saw Uncle Arnold's head appear, a bit like that scene in Alien.

"Not much to this bloke," he said. "Been in his head… full of bullshit as far as I can see. You'll never get a fair hearing from him. Wait a minute, I'll try something…"

Throughout all this, the psychiatrist had been watching me very carefully, completely oblivious to the ghostly head sticking out of his chest. He opened his mouth to say something and then stopped. "Wait…" he finally managed to say. He looked down at his chest. Uncle Arnold's head spun 180 degrees to look at him. "Mornin' lad," he said with such pleasantry that I felt that if he'd been wearing a hat he would have doffed it. "Now then, leave my nephew alone!"

I'll give the psychiatrist his due… he held his ground. "What is this?" he said. "How have you done this? Is it hypnosis?"

I put up my hands and shook my head. "Even I didn't know they could do that. Nothing to do with me." The psychiatrist tried to touch Uncle Arnold's head – his hand passed straight through. Uncle Arnold shook his head. "Tell you what," he said. "You accept that my nephew can see dead people and I'll stop bothering you. If you don't…" He left the sentence hanging. Uncle Arnold emerged from the psychiatrist's body and stood in front of him. "Deal?"

The psychiatrist shakily put out a hand to shake on it. Uncle Arnold looked at it, then the psychiatrist's face. "Don't be silly," he said, and disappeared.

The next few hours were rather surreal. The psychiatrist left the room I was in after hurriedly making some proper notes this time. Then several doctors came in, checked me over and nodded amongst themselves.

Finally, some suited wonk came in with some papers for me to sign, saying that I was free to go and that I wouldn't hold anyone responsible blah blah blah… So twelve hours after being arrested in a churchyard talking to the residents I was walking down the street towards the bus stop. I looked to my left and saw a procession of dead people walking beside me, Uncle Albert at their head. "Well done, lad," he said. "I told some of my friends what had happened… appalled, they were. So we've decided to stage a protest march." There was a lot of head nodding amongst the dead – some of them even carried placards, with slogans like 'Dead yes gone no' and so on. It was only then that I began to notice the reaction of ordinary, living people around me. "See?" said Uncle Arnold. "That's the problem the living have! Dead and that's it. Well, I think that's about to change." As I marched on with all my dead friends, I realised things would have to change. This was no zombie uprising, this was just another group of angry citizens demanding their civil rights!

Ellie's Fairy Wood

By Kate Booth

The chainsaw had bitten through more than the peace in Blyth Woodland that autumn day.

The old tree had stood for over four hundred years, but the company of mushrooms had been its final death knoll. The heart wood had softened, and the insects had burrowed. Woodpeckers had pecked and fed on these. They reared their young in this hole and safe from wind and rain, they grew and flew the roost. All this company made the tree busy, and the tree was growing as the old wood and leaves gave back it nutrients to go on building new wood. Flickers of sunlight and leaves waving in the canopy made joyful patterns, and a blissful atmosphere for walking humans.

The children could see more though. The champions of the wood had moved in. Fairies, as dainty as petals; drifted across the clearing. Flying on the breeze, or were they flying with wings? The hole in the oak was their destination, their home.

The children could see the fairies, and enjoyed their dancing, and whirling colours. They knew Amber, and Jet, as well as Fleet but above all Candytuft. Candytuft was the oldest and wisest of the Fairies. She remembered the acorn, which had been planted and it grew into this beautiful oak over hundreds of years. Her life had always depended on the trees. The fairies helped to sort the colours in the leaves, so that they faded in the cool autumn air: from greens to yellows, oranges and reds giving a magical display. Rain water with sunlight would throw these colours up, into rainbows in the sky. Fairies grew in the energy from the trees as they shut down their leaves to survive winter.

Flowers from the spring through the whole of the summer were the main work and food of the fairy folk: Bluebells, and Periwinkles, Rosy

Garlic, Sage and Mint. As the leaves were bruised by foot fall, or hit by rain drops, they would give off their smells. Humans valued these plants because these smells would make food smell and taste good. Fairies flew on these perfumes and grew on their nectar. Best of all the holes in the timber gave fairies sanctuary from falling feet, rain and hailstones. Even snow was too much for the fairies. In winter there was little colour, few plants to care for, or fragrant smells and nectar to cheer their days. So they slept curled away from the cold. They liked to join a mouse or two, or even a hedgehog on the short days of winter.

The lucky folk who could see the fairy flickers on sunny days and were also aware of the darker side of woodland folk. The small folk that people had call Dwarves, did the dirty work, breaking down old vegetation, or dead animals. They worked with maggots, insect larvae, and the ever present bacterial and fungal strands. This network of fine tubes would pick up the nutrients from decaying plants, leaves, flowers and the dead animals gave over their useful parts. There was nothing wasted, the Dwarves made sure of that.

In modern times Dwarves preferred to be known as Morphs.

Their building blocks from broken down woodland were led to the new spring growth. Morphs made the bulbs push up strong shoots and Flowers. Blue bells were multiplying, and the Brambles were growing long wandering tendrils. Battles were acted out by the new growth underground. Morphs battled Morphs for the use of these precious woodland parts. Some of the new plants were armoured with spikes, thorns or poisons. But the tender plants relied on the protection of the Morphs, who would fight off the damaging grazers, like slugs and snails. Morphs brought in the predators, riding birds as sport was a great pastime. Dark shadows in rustling leaf litter, thrushes fighting for crawling decomposers, or being fended off by the Morphs. But the dark side of the Morphs were far from being enemies with the fairy world. The threat of tree felling by man had to be planned for by Morphs and fairies together.

Main Points of Meeting.

- ❖ No one to be hurt; so fairies and small people to be on guard.
- ❖ Find a new "Safe house" for Candytuft and her Fairy family.
- ❖ Share moving to new House. WHEN? As soon as possible.
- ❖ Plant seeds for replacement trees, transfer magic, and history from the old tree. Fairy work.

- ❖ Have a Fairy and Morph party , bring what you can
- ❖ Enjoy the Company and spread your young

So that was what happened.

The New House was found on the other side of the Dip so it was further away from the Human path and their erratic behaviour. The New Home Tree was middle aged, and it already had a good hole in one side; great for moving in and out. No established Fairies or large animals. The Morphs checked that the new Tree was already well served by micro morphs. Morphs, breaking down old leaves and tree parts, and releasing lots of nutrients for all the whole woodland: Morphs, Fairies, plants and animals of all sizes.

All Good. The Move was on.

The next day, there was a day of shuffling Candytuft's treasures to the New Tree. Seeds, spores and her happy glowing memory moments which were picked up and spread by the smallest fairies. The mushrooms had just come into fruiting bodies to spore, so some of their energy was going to come with Candytuft when she moved into the New Tree.

Tomorrow the men had said, and they were as good as their word.

The buzz of the chainsaw started early, the vibrations travelled through the ground, through the air and through the old tree. The men had to saw for ages: a wedge of wood out one of the far side, and then a second slice, and a third on the weak side.

And then her old oak home fell, with a crash of snapping branches and a cloud of fungal spores. Oh what a show, the Morphs and fairies all cheered from their perches in the New Tree, across the wood.

The party that night was wonderfully happy, so I am told.

And the small girl called Ellie was walking with her father John in the wood in Blyth a few days later. He had always known stories from the fairy world, so he took a picture of the fairy forest. And they told this to their wider family, and said how special it was.

Let's keep folk stories alive and value the imaginations of our children!

Daughters of Eden

By Margaret Kerswell

"The Daughters of Eden need your help," came the call from the woman standing on the street that Saturday afternoon, almost five years ago.

"Who are the Daughters of Eden?" I asked my mother as we carried on walking. I noticed she'd quickened her pace as we passed the woman.

"Some crackpot group you need to stay away from!" she said. Her tone told me that was the last she wanted to hear of it, but her response only served to make me more curious.

What made them crackpots? Why should I stay away from them? One look at my mother's face told me I'd be pushing my luck to ask, but, I thought, Aunt Debbie would tell me more. I'd go visit her.

Later that day I walked into my Aunt Debbie's studio apartment. She was my mother's sister and looking at them you could tell, but their natures were polar opposites. I loved my mother dearly but she was a naturally uptight kind of person, whereas Aunt Debbie was so laid back she was horizontal.

"Hi Aunt D," I said as I walked in to her kitchen area and perched on a high stool.

"Hello Honey," Aunt Debbie responded looking up with a huge welcoming smile on her face. "What you up to?" she asked.

"Not much," I replied, trying to sound casual

I looked over at my Aunt who sat back in her seat and raised her eyebrows. I could almost hear her saying, "Yeah right!"

I smiled at her sheepishly.

"Aunt Debbie," I said, "can I ask you something?"

My Aunt sat up straighter. "Of course you can, sweetheart, what's up?"

"Well," I began, "on Saturday me and Mum were up the street and there was a woman by Johnstone's Square. She was shouting 'The Daughters of Eden need your help'." Aunt Debbie nodded. "Who are the Daughters of Eden?" I finished and looking my Aunt straight in the eye.

Slowly Aunt Debbie got up, made her way to the sink and got a drink of water.

"Have you asked your Mum about this?" she enquired. I nodded and Aunt Debbie raised her eyebrows once again.

"I did," I protested at her 'don't believe you' look. "I asked Mum and she just said they were 'some crackpot group' and I should 'stay away' from them."

Aunt Debbie nodded. "That's typical of my sister that is - don't explain anything just tell you to stay away. Does she not realise it just makes you more interested?!" She shook her head a little.

"Well, that's what she said and I *am* interested," I said. "Who are they, Aunt D?"

"She's right," Aunt Debbie said as she sat back down opposite me. "They are a bunch of crackpots and you should indeed stay away from them."

"But why?" I began, my Aunt held up her hand to stop me.

"Have you ever heard of a cult?" Aunt Debbie asked. I probably looked confused. Yes, I knew what a cult was, but surely there wouldn't be anything like that in our little town. I nodded.

"Well, that is exactly what The Daughters of Eden are," she said matter of factly. "They're a cult who prey on vulnerable young girls. Give them a wide berth sweetheart; you don't want to be sucked in."

Aunt Debbie sounded a little funny, her tone was strange but I couldn't quite... then it struck me. My Aunt was scared.

I nodded, the worried look on my favourite Aunt's face was enough for me to realise she was very serious.

"I'm Sorry Aunt D, I mean, I just wondered and well, Mum wouldn't tell me, and well, I didn't mean to upset you. Sorry," I stammered.

"It's OK sweetheart," Aunt Debbie said, moving next to me so she could give me a hug. "I'm not upset, I just worry. I've seen what these people can do to their followers. It scares me to think that they're recruiting again and you could be enticed to get involved. Please promise me you'll stay away from them."

I nodded my head. "I promise Aunt Debbie, I'll stay away from them," I said and at that moment I honestly meant it. In fact I don't think I'd ever meant anything more in my life.

But here I am, four years later, sat in the Daughters of Eden 'recruitment' office, trying to smile and nod in all the right places.

Don't worry though I'm not here because I want to join, NO. I want my friend back!

"So, you're interested in joining us?" The bespectacled lady sitting over the desk from me asked.

No, I thought not a hope in hell's chance, but I found myself smiling sweetly, saying, "Why yes, it would be an honour. A friend of mine, Sarah Hall, became involved with you about a year ago. Before she moved away she had nothing but good things to say. So I thought I'd bite the bullet, so to speak, and see for myself." I gave her the best sincere smile I could fake.

"Ahh yes, Sarah, she's a lovely girl," said Miss Spectacles. Yes, I thought, she's bought it! "I have of course spoken to Sarah about you and she's given you a glowing reference. So, providing you can meet our other criteria and guide lines it would be a pleasure to have you," she finished with her own overly friendly smile. She rose from her chair and left the room without another word.

I sat in that room for twenty minutes on my own waiting for her to return. When she did, eventually, she wasn't alone. Following behind her were two straight faced ladies wearing white coats. They both looked at me, then the three of them spoke in hushed tones for a moment, finally one turned back to me.

"Please follow us," she said with a small smile.

I stood, the apprehension must have shown on my face because Miss Spectacles spoke to me saying, "There's nothing to worry about. It's just a quick medical, everyone has one"

This revelation didn't make me feel any better - a medical. I had no idea this was going to be so intrusive. Still I needed access to Sarah and this looked to be my only way in, so I followed the women in white coats.

I was led down the corridor to a brightly lit room. It was pretty much empty except for a chair, a wheeled trolley and a hospital style bed. The women stepped aside for me to enter, one handed me a sheet of A4 paper with questions on and a black biro saying simply, "Answer honestly please." The other said, "When you're finished please remove all your clothes and put on the gown provided. We will return shortly," then they both left.

I stood a little disbelievingly. What the hell? I thought what kind of medical was this? I'd half expected my weight and height checked, but by the looks of this it was going to be in-depth.

I took the sheet of questions and sat on the chair, first things first I thought, let's get this filled in….

Q1 Have you ever had sexual intercourse?

What? No name? Age? Address questions? Straight into questions about my sexual relationships? What difference did that make to anyone? I toyed with the idea of just writing 'None of your bloody business!' Then I thought of Sarah, these people were obviously off their trollies, I needed to find her and get her out! So, I ticked the 'yes' box. I'm pretty sure they'd struggle to find an over eighteen who hadn't had sex nowadays!

Q2 Do you have or have you ever had any of the following? (tick all that apply)

> *HIV*
>
> *AIDS*
>
> *SYPHILIS*
>
> *HERPES*
>
> *GONORRHEA*

These questions were getting worse! What on earth had Sarah gotten herself into?

I carried on answering the questions all the time wondering what on earth they needed this kind of information for. I mean really, who needs to know how many different sexual partners I've had?

When I'd finished, I undressed and put on the open backed hospital gown I'd been left and waited.

After a short while my two 'friends' in white coats returned and there followed one of the most traumatising in-depth examinations I've ever endured. They spoke very little other than to 'tell' me, *not* ask me, to stand or lie in certain positions etc. When they'd finished I was told to dress and follow them to yet another sparsely decorated room. Where once on my own I couldn't help but sob: I felt totally violated. Even now I still feel physically sick at the thought of that day: passing years have done very little to alleviate the horror of it all.

I must have waited for the best part of an hour before Miss Spectacles entered the room. At least I suppose it gave me a chance to compose myself for whatever came next.

When she came in Miss Spectacles brought with her a tray containing a jug of ice cold water and two glasses. The water was a welcome relief to my burning throat. I drank my first glass like I'd not had water for days, Miss Spectacles raised her eyebrows as I poured a second glass and settled sipping it politely.

"Well," she said clearing her throat. "I'm pleased to say you've passed your medical and you fit our criteria." She smiled her over friendly smile again. "So, I'd like to welcome you to join us."

Inside I felt physically sick. Outwardly I smiled the biggest smile I could muster and said, "That's fantastic news, I'm so honoured and look forward to working with you."

What happened to Jasper?

By Linda Jobling

Marjorie lived alone, miles from her nearest neighbour, along a muddy track that went nowhere but to a ramshackle rough whitewashed house. Its grey, slated roof barely kept out the howling wind and rain, with tiles missing and others hanging on by a thread. The glass window panes had long been broken and she'd carefully cut cardboard to fit each missing piece, crisscrossing them with black tape. Her cats could come and go as they pleased through holes in the remaining broken panes.

Walkers would sometimes pass by and she could often be seen with her head peeking out of the metal window frame, with her straggly dyed black hair and her bright red lips, shouting obscenities as they passed. Once a group of pony trekkers passed her door and disturbed her peace. "Bloody pony trekkers," she used to say. "Some peasants in anoraks and pumps, we all know the sort."

Marjorie was known in the village as the 'witch' with extraordinary powers. She could put a fear into anyone who ridiculed her. Her face was brown and weathered with deep wrinkles that ran down both sides of her long pointed nose. Her back was bent from years of carrying heavy shopping and she lived a world divorced from the one she had known in her childhood.

Born to wealthy parents she had had the best of everything, but now chose to live the life of a hermit, with her cats and dogs and Jasper the ram. Marjorie had nurtured and fed him from the day he was born. Left on the field when his mother died and William the farmer had neither the time nor the expensive milk needed to keep him alive, Marjorie gave Jasper all the love and attention only a mother could give a child. Jasper was left to roam wherever he pleased. He was her world.

Marjorie had long forgotten what it was like to sleep on a bed. Sleeping on a small settee, fully clothed in a dusty room strewn with newspapers, half chewed boxes and her magazines; The county life, The Field, The Lady and other expensive books dating back many years.

In the small dark kitchen, amongst the clutter, an easel took pride of place where she spent hours painting, transporting herself to another world, the world of wealth and childhood spent in Argentina where her father worked on the railway. They had servants and maids and a tutor would call twice a week to teach her Latin, French and arithmetic. She was also taught play the piano and harp.

Marjorie still held an air of snobbery: she had rejected all her wealth and given her share of the family home in London to her siblings and in return they gave her a monthly allowance.

Her evenings were spent on her Ouija board and she fascinated the locals by predicting the future. Marjorie's lonely existence with her animals gave her a contented and happy life until the beginning of spring 1949.

Spring had arrived after long cruel months of snow and ice, leaving remnants of its grip with pockets of snow clearly visible on the hillside. Not even the warm rays of sunshine that woke Marjorie that morning could heat up the cold damp room she slept in. She yawned and sat up thinking of the day ahead before venturing out into the cold. The forlorn cry of a bird broke the silence. A shiver went down her spine. "A sign of death," she thought.

With aching bones she opened the door to face the bitter wind. The snow on the lane outside was trodden down leaving a thick crust of pale grey ice. Cautiously she made her way down the path to the bar, crunching the snow beneath her feet, her teeth chattering uncontrollably as she went. The air was clean and sharp, leaving a trail of vapour as she breathed. Marjorie gathered the remaining hay from the barn and bundled it under her arm to feed Jasper.

"Jasper, Jasper," she called in her high pitched voice. He usually came running. Marjorie strained her eyes against the stark grey sky, blinking in rapid succession. She reached in her pocket to wipe her watery eyes scanning the field and hedgerows, straining to see where Jasper might be.

"Jasper, Jaaasper," she called, her voice becoming more hysterical.

There was no response.

Marjorie rested on a piece of log when a strange fear gripped her heart: holding back the tears she looked around again. Brushing the wispy hair from her face she slowly made her way around the field, constantly calling out his name and trying to keep calm. Marjorie climbed over the style and stood looking around all the remaining fields. To her horror there wasn't a sheep to be seen. A sharp pain ripped through her heart as if she had been stabbed. Marjorie made her way back to her cottage, totally fatigued. She fumbled around for her matches to light her paraffin stove, then she warmed her hands, before breaking the thin layer of ice that covered her water tub outside. Marjorie filled her kettle and lay on the settee, tears now coursing down her cheeks as she waited for the kettle to boil. Deep in thought, trying to make sense of what had happened to Jasper, she reached for her Ouija board and placed it on the table with an upturned glass.

The glass started to move: DEAD

"Dead? How? Where? When?" So many questions – no answers.

The glass moved again: MEAT

DEAD MEAT? Whatever could that mean?

So many thoughts went through her mind. It's Monday, she thought, Market Day. A strange fear gripped her heart. He must have strayed to William's field and been taken to market with the rest of the sheep. Marjorie was grief-stricken.

She hastily pulled on her Wellington boots, wrapped herself in her warm coat and woollen hat and made her way across the slippery field. Her Wellington boots squelched in the muddy ruts as she laboured slowly towards William's farm. It was now early evening and the light was fading fast. Marjorie looked up as a small, white, fluffy cloud drifted by on the freshening wind. "It looks just like Jasper," she thought as she plodded on.

In the distance she could see the large farmhouse with its imposing buildings. Her sense of foreboding deepened as she quickened her pace, eventually reaching the grey door. With her cold, weathered fingers she clutched the heavy knocker and hammered with fury on the heavy door. She was met by a very surprised William.

Marjorie blurted out her story.

"Don't you come here accusing me of taking your bloody Jasper, if you don't keep him under control and stop him coming into my field. How the hell do you expect me to spot him amongst the sheep I rounded up today? How do you know that he was amongst the sheep that went to market anyway?" William asked, harshly.

Through her tears and intermittent sobs she attempted to say, "My Ouija board told me last night."

"Bugger off from here and don't come accusing me of stealing your stupid ram. Don't set foot on this farm again, talking such bloody nonsense. Ouija board indeed!" In his anger William slammed the door in his face. Marjorie was incensed.

Flushed and angry she slowly made her way home, mumbling and talking to herself, her legs getting heavier with every step she took. "William will wish he had never seen or heard of me," she thought. "I will sort him out when I get home…"

Midnight Sun

By Harry Lane

As dawn's first flush touches the sky and birdsong heralds the approaching day, I lie still. As the deer runs and dogs bark and children open their blue eyes, I lie still. As hope spreads across the land and footsteps stride out anew, I lie still. Safe and at peace in the cold darkness: face bloated, hair dark and that pulse that can scarce be detected.

As that golden disc climbs higher and the day picks up its heartbeat, I remember. I remember times long past when we were people of importance, looked up to, respected. Now we are outcasts, driven from our homelands, pursued by heathens. Always we are driven on, never allowed to rest. Chased by flaming brands and burning crosses, I head North.

It is not the day but the night I look forward to. When the sun is replaced by his sister the moon. This is my time, our time, when the heartbeat quickens and the limbs begin to move. To stand alert and fresh in that cold air and watch the sun set. As ever, I head North, toward new lands where a fresh start awaits and people do not know us.

I have travelled far and waited long for this, to stand looking down on that small market town hidden deep in the pine forest. There are many such as this. The light fading, the moon about to rise, I breathe deep and feel at peace.

"What's wrong?" Something has changed, but what?

A tingling in my fingers and arms, my legs begin to tremble. A trickle down my back like water. Sweat, but I never sweat. My forehead and hair are damp. Perspiration. My skin starts to feel like it's on fire, the odd thermal of smoke rising up through my clothes. The night, it's getting lighter, brighter. I fall to my knees unable to breathe, my chest is on fire and as my face begins to melt, I realise: this is December, this is Norway and this is the land of the midnight sun.

He kinda liked the feeling, so shiny and smooth in his hand...

By Martin Booth

Caleb put his hand into his pocket and pulled out some crumpled bills. Although he knew exactly how much money he had he counted it again carefully... just to make sure. Two years of working odd jobs, some hired fieldwork and tenderfoot on a cattle drive had earned him almost $80, all with an aim in mind.

Just to be sure, Caleb looked at the money in his hand again: thirty four dollars and a few cents. More than enough. He pushed the store door open and went into the cool interior. The proprietor smiled at the young man. "Mornin' Caleb, you alright?"

"Yes thanks, Mr Simmons. I've come to spend some money."

Simmons smiled again. He had known Caleb since he'd been born and liked the lad... he could be a bit impetuous at times, but a hard worker. "So, what can I get you, young man?"

"That Colt revolver in the display case, Mr Simmons."

There was silence in the shop for a few seconds, then Simmons put his head on one side. "Now then, Caleb, what you be wantin' that for?"

Caleb squared his shoulders. "I went on that cattle drive last spring, Mr. Simmons. That's what I want to do, so I need a gun... the other hands carry one."

"All right, Caleb," said Simmons, "I'll get it out for you." He went to the display case and unlocked it. The he lifted out the pistol, turned it in his hand so the handle was towards Caleb and handed it over. The young man took hold of it. After wanting... desiring the pistol for so long, now he was actually holding it he didn't really know what to do. Simmons' brow furrowed. "Caleb... Caleb! Can you use a gun?"

Caleb gripped the butt tightly. "I'll learn. One of the hands on the trail let me shoot at some cans."

"Hit any?"

"After I practice I will," said Caleb. He pulled the hammer back and pulled the trigger, hearing the click as the hammer fell onto an empty space where the cartridge would be. Simmons took the gun back from Caleb. "If you want to use a gun, you need to know how to shoot but more importantly, *when* to shoot. Too many men been killed when a word would have done. Now watch."

With practiced fingers, Simmons pulled the hammer back to half cock, unlocked the cylinder and spun it, working the ejector to show Caleb how to clear the empty cartridge cases from the weapon. Then he let the hammer down and handed it back to Caleb. "Hold it out," he said.

Caleb held the Colt at arm's length and sighted along the barrel. It wobbled in his hand and he lowered it. "It's heavy," he said, feeling slightly foolish.

"Weighs a tad under two and a half pounds, fully loaded. Need strength in your arm, boy, to use that."

"I'll work on it," said Caleb. "How much is it?"

Simmons looked Caleb in the eye. "It's thirty dollars, son. And more for a box of cartridges."

"I got that," said Caleb.

Simmons put the gun down on the counter. "Look, son, if you want to be a cowpoke, good for you. It's hard work, long hours in the saddle but the money's good. And most hands don't even carry one of these." He gestured towards the Colt. "Get yourself a decent rifle. Got a new Winchester .44 over there for the same price."

Caleb was momentarily undecided. He knew that almost all cowhands did indeed carry a rifle on their saddle, but some carried a pistol as well, and Caleb was young enough to be impressed by that. "No," he said, "I want the Colt."

"How many shells?"

"Er, fifty."

Simmons reached under the counter and took out a box of cartridges. "Here." Caleb went to pick them up and dropped them back onto the counter. "Heavy, ain't they? Weigh more than the gun, Caleb. You strong enough to even carry them out the store? And what you gonna carry that gun in? Walk around the streets with that in your hand and you'll be dead or in gaol before you reach the end of Main Street."

Caleb was starting to feel angry. He'd wanted this gun for almost two years. In his imagination, he'd walked into the shop, bought the pistol, carried it home and within a few days been a crack shot. Now he was learning that it was a lot more difficult that he'd ever thought. Simmons looked at the young man standing in front of him. He took in a deep breath and let it out slowly. "Tell you what, Caleb," he said. "Go home now – safely – and get your daddy's rifle. Tell him I said so. Do some practice with that in the woods and I'll come out tonight with this Colt and that new Winchester." He reached under the counter again and handed Caleb a dozen cartridges. "Here. These'll fit that rifle. We'll talk it through with your pa and you can decide then. If you still want the Colt I'll show you how to use it properly. That way you might just survive long enough to get on that cattle drive." He paused for a minute and continued. "You can even have a holster for it – pay me after your next drive."

Inside, Caleb was relieved but outside he couldn't let it show. "OK, Mr Simmons. I'll take you up on that offer," he said, slipping the cartridges into his pocket. "Until later." He tipped his hat the way he'd seen others do and walked to the door. Caleb was about to open it when Simmons stopped him. "I know you want to be a cowhand, Caleb," he said, "but most hands I know never use their guns from one year's end to the next. Remember that. Wave a gun around and someone better and faster than you will kill you."

But his final words were drowned out by the slam of the door as it closed behind the young boy hoping soon to be a man.

Cabinet Pussy-cat

By Daniel Brown

Glynis sat in the bay window of her front room, staring at the cars passing down the road outside her bungalow. The traffic had calmed down in recent months since the local council had placed speed bumps, but the lure of a short-cut to the high street was still too much for a lot of motorists to ignore. Tom would have enjoyed seeing the speed bumps placed, having campaigned for so many years to have something done about the way people would tear up and down their street at break neck pace, for no other reason than to shave a minute or two off their journey to or from the local supermarket.

The same supermarket that had driven Tom out of business ten years earlier. Not that they had any reason to be bitter, Tom was ready to retire anyway and they had no children to pass the little butcher's shop on to. They had always put a little away each week and after selling the shop and the three bedroomed house they had bought when they first married, anticipating children who never came, they had bought their little bungalow and the remainder made for a nice little pension. All told their retirement was shaping up to be a nice experience for both of them.

Instead, she had let her poor Tom down. Barely two months after they retired she had a massive stroke, losing all mobility in her left side. Worse than that though, she had lost forever the ability to express herself with speech. The words would line themselves up in her head, as nice as you like, but as soon as she opened her mouth out would pour a string of nonsense; words and phrases that bore no resemblance to intelligent speech, let alone the sentence she was trying articulate. Every day after that her heart had broken a little further, ashamed for the fact that Tom, far from relaxing and enjoying his final years on earth, found himself burdened with a gibbering, self-soiling old cripple. Tom would never have it that way, of course, always insisting that she was the main reason he got up in the mornings, just like every day since she had first walked into his dad's butcher's shop so many years before.

Every day thereafter would follow the same routine. After waking up Tom would lift her onto her commode and leave the room, waiting patiently for her to shout to signal she had finished. Once he had heard the call he would come back in and gently wipe her clean, before lifting her into her wheelchair as delicately as a man holding a new-born baby. Being Tom, of course, there would often follow a little joke about liking any chance to touch between her legs, but Glynis knew those kinds of thought never passed through his mind when he was helping her with the toilet. Sometimes she wished that they would, since they had always been... *healthy,* in that respect, right up until she had the stroke. She had tried telling him how she felt but the words she longed for would never come out. The closest she ever came to it was a string of obscenities that had made Tom blush, having never heard that kind of language from his wife, a woman who had previously never sworn properly in fifty three years together. She had tried using her writing pad to ask him once, since she could still write as clearly as ever, but he had just smiled at her and told her he was happy to wait until she was a little better.

Glynis had never found out if he meant what he had said, or if he was just repulsed at the idea of doing those things they had enjoyed so much with the wreck she felt she'd become. So many times she had wanted to ask him, burning to know the reason a man who had always been so *enthusiastic* about their physical relationship was now so reticent. A few times a week she would put pen to paper, trying to phrase the question properly, but every time her courage deserted her. She would imagine herself looking at him as he read her notepad and seeing a look of revulsion on his face, a flicker of some deeply hidden emotion in his eyes that would reveal what she lived in terror of knowing. That she disgusted him, that he felt every ounce of the utter bloody repulsiveness she herself felt at the loss of her independence, trapped in a body that no longer worked and reliant on the one man on earth she felt it was her duty to look after as he approached his dotage.

Other than that one niggling doubt, Tom had been a better husband than she could ever have dared to ask for. He had never once treated her like an idiot, never talked down to her and never showed even the slightest hint of weariness at the constant twenty four hour care she had needed in those early days of her long, slow recovery. He would take her out every day, rain or shine, to do the things they had always done together. They would go shopping, or to the cinema; he would take her to her favourite café for lunch and then on to the local park to watch the bowls matches or to admire the floral displays the town was so well known for. She would stare at the flowers, enchanted by their beauty, the riot of colours and scents always a source of joy to a woman who had spent most of her working life surrounded by raw meat and the ever-present smell of offal and dead flesh. In her entranced state she would be unable to hold her usual self-imposed silence and try to express her delight aloud. She would concentrate, fiercely focusing all of her will on saying just two little words; "Beautiful flowers", but the words she grasped for never came. Her addled brain would let her down every time and instead out of her mouth would come "Cabinet pussy-cat", the one consistent phrase in her otherwise hopelessly muddled vocabulary.

On those occasions Tom would keep his face deadpan and say something like "Very cabinet indeed." or "Funny place to keep a cat." If anyone else had tried that she would have used her good hand to scratch their eyes out, but that had always been Tom's way. Brush things off with a joke, laugh at everything. There was no-one else, anywhere in the world who could make her laugh at the pathetic wretch she felt herself to be and it was during those times together that she felt she loved him so much her heart would burst; shatter into a million little pieces at the pain she was sure he was masking with his jokes and asides, but it didn't. Instead Tom's heart did and just as she was beginning to accept her circumstances, for the first time in her life she was alone.

Even after five years of attempting to adjust to life on her own, she missed Tom with as much passion and fearsome agony as the very first morning after the heart attack had taken him from her.

She thought she had felt shame about her condition before, but after Tom's tender ministrations and justifiable expression of faint distaste, seeing the look of brusque efficiency on the face of the care attendant sent out by social services four times a day to help with her toilet needs was almost more than she could bear. Being helped with your needs by the man you adored and had known for almost a lifetime was embarrassing, being helped by someone you didn't know and who treat you as just one more doddery old fool who couldn't go for a piddle on her own was an exercise in degradation. She had redoubled her efforts to improve her state of dependence, physiotherapy, speech therapy and occupational therapy had all been undertaken with renewed vigour, and while physiotherapy was the only area where any great improvement was made, it was enough that with the help of her occupational therapist she was able to use the toilet on her own, cook her own meals again and live a life relatively free of other people's interference. Free, that is, apart from Helen.

Helen with her sniping and her vicious tongue. Helen, who could cut through Glynis' fragile self-confidence with one well-chosen remark, leaving her once again the frightened and lonely woman she had been after Tom's death. It was Helen who had gotten on so well with the home help that the gullible woman had taken to talking down at Glynis in the same pitying, mock cheerful tone that made her nerves jangle every time Helen spoke to her. It was Helen who had called the ambulance three years ago when Glynis had a heart attack of her own, saving her life and delaying her reunion with Tom. Helen was all of that, and she was coming over for coffee.

Sighing heavily, she moved the controls of her electric wheelchair, turning away from the window and back into the living room proper, glancing up at the mantle as she did so towards where Tom's ashes rested. She moved past the sofa they had chosen together getting ready for the big move into their small house; past the old fashioned dark mahogany sideboard that was far too big for the tiny living room, a wedding gift from her mother that neither of them had the heart to get rid of, the top cluttered with photos and keepsakes. Their wedding pictures, photos of holidays and family get-togethers, from their honeymoon as youngsters through middle age and right up to the night of her late husband's retirement party.

As she moved into the kitchen, she pressed the switch down on the kettle in preparation for the visit of her neighbour for her habitual coffee and bourbon cream biscuits, the same routine as almost every morning for the past nine years since Helen had bought the bungalow next to hers. Reaching into the cupboard for the cups, the coffee the milk powder and everything else she knew her friend needed in her brew. Helen was very particular in her tastes, lashing out viciously with her tongue if her meticulous standards weren't met by all she encountered. Sometimes Glynis wondered why the woman bothered with other people at all when her expectations were always let down so appallingly.

She had always been a bit demanding, not the easiest of company to keep at the best of times, but since Tom had died she had really shown her true colours, berating Glynis at every turn. Constantly reminding her of how useless she had become, she would spend sometimes an hour or more telling Glynis how much she pitied her, how she was only living half a life and that in itself wasn't much to write home about; how she was dependent on other people's good will for the mostly independent life she was living. In order to illustrate her point she would often move Glynis' things around at random, placing precious objects where she couldn't retrieve them herself and would have to ask Helen to put them back for her. Several months ago she had picked Tom's ashes from their place on the mantle-piece and put them onto the high shelf built into the corner of the room nearest the window, leaving them balancing precariously on the edge where the slightest vibration could send them crashing to the floor.

In her panic Glynis had forgotten all about the writing pad around her neck, breaking her self-imposed vow of silence and shouting at Helen to lift them down immediately.

"Violin the paper, speaker box button tight! Orange reflectors!" Helen had stared at her, shocked momentarily into silence by the vehemence in Glynis' voice. Then she had started to laugh, that patronizing little snort she made whenever she was describing somebody else's shortcomings.

"Would you listen to yourself Glynis? You sound completely ridiculous. If I ever end up in the state you're in I'll do away with myself pretty bloody sharp-ish. There's no way I'm letting myself end up the pathetic mess you're in, I'll tell you that for nothing!" Helen had reached up for the ashes then, her little victory complete, and restoring them to pride of place above the fire. "Don't worry, pet. Your hubby's ashes are safe and sound, you poor little thing." Glynis had been so anxious and angry that she had to take one of her heart tablets as soon as she saw Tom put safely back where he belonged. Even thinking back on the incident now, she could feel her heartbeat skipping in her remembered panic.

The kettle clicked loudly in the silent kitchen, bringing Glynis out of her reverie. She looked at the digital clock on the cooker and saw the time was eleven twenty nine. She poured the still boiling water into the cups, stirring Helen's coffee thoroughly to dissolve every last little grain in her mug before seeing to her own cup of lemon tea. No sooner were the drinks prepared, when she heard the front door open. She could hear Helen's heavy breathing, even through two rooms and the hallway. Her neighbour wasn't usually one for pointing out faults, at least not in herself, but she cheerfully owned up to a total inability to give up a sixty a day cigarette habit.

Glynis looked around as her neighbour bustled her way through the living room, puffing and blowing outrageously as she went. Helen came into the kitchen, red faced and sweating slightly from the walk up, then straight back down two deceptively long garden paths. She leaned down and grabbed from the lowered work surface, nodding a curt thank you at Glynis as she did so, then turned around and hurried back into the living room to put her, rather large, backside into the armchair beside the window. Glynis put her tea and the packet of biscuits onto the tray attached to her wheelchair and manoeuvred herself into the other room, bracing herself to listen to her guest carp and moan about every subject that came into her nasty little mind.

Helen had already lit up a cigarette when Glynis arrived at her habitual parking spot and was blowing smoke around herself with a proprietary air. She waited patiently for her guest to get her breath back, then gestured towards Helen and raised her eyebrows.

"I'm fine, thanks for asking, pet. How are you today?" Glynis waved her hand in the universal gesture for "so-so". Helen nodded perfunctorily, indicating to Glynis that her part in the conversation was over. She flicked her cigarette ash onto the floor, rubbed it in with her foot and muttered "Good for the carpet, isn't it?" Glynis looked down at the patch of darkened weave, where her neighbour had done that every day for years. She wondered briefly, where exactly Helen had picked up that pearl of carpet care wisdom. Perhaps her own carpets were covered with grey patches like mildew or creeping damp. If that was so, she was pleased that Helen wasn't responsible for the cleaning duties in *her* house. The large harridan took a gulp of her still steaming coffee and Glynis thought the woman's mouth must be coated with asbestos.

"The coffee's bitter today isn't it? Just because you don't drink it yourself, doesn't mean you can't replace it when it goes stale." Matronly disapproval was written all over Helen's face. Glynis reached for the writing pad dangling around her neck but the other woman waved her hand dismissively.

"There's no need to apologise, pet. I wouldn't expect someone who's damned near a vegetable to remember everything." She managed to keep her face impassive, saying to herself that she was actually going to write "Choke on it, you fat old witch!", still there was no sense in winding her up just yet. Two more gulps and the coffee was gone, Helen placing the empty cup on the floor beside her feet. She looked over at Glynis, her face adopting the usual look of spiteful glee reserved for when she was about to impart some particularly nasty piece of gossip.

Helen launched into a tirade against Alan Jamieson from just down the road who, according to the rumours, was having a fling with the young woman who drove the library van, but Glynis was only half listening. She was lost in her own thoughts, wondering whether the home help was going to call at her usual time of between three o'clock and three thirty. She certainly hoped so, as she had a few things she wanted to say to her neighbour in privacy and really couldn't be having with any interruptions.

She let Helen prattle on for a while, maybe five minutes, staying serene as the venomous words washed over her, paying close attention to the other woman's face. It didn't take long, Helen's face got progressively paler as her monologue went on. Sweat was dripping out of every pore on her face and her eyes became wider and less focused with every passing second. Her hand fluttered to her chest, while a panicky expression crossed her face. Glynis smiled at her discomfort, watching dispassionately as Helen tried to stand up, tottered a few steps away from the armchair and collapsed backwards, sprawling face down, right on that god awful stain she had made with years of abuse by cigarette ash.

That'll be the digitalis- thought Glynis. She knew *exactly* what her neighbour needed in her brew. Ever since that business with Tom's ashes she had saved one out of every three capsules that she was supposed to take, carefully emptying them into a food bag that she stored at the back of her cutlery drawer. She didn't know exactly how many were needed for a fatal dose, but once she thought she had enough she emptied the bag into Helen's mug, stirring it in like coffee-mate. Looking down at the fat harridan now, she was pretty sure she could have given her half the amount and still got the same effect. Still, her Tom had always told her, "Too much of something is far better than not enough. Except syphilis." She smiled at the memory of his words. Always the joker.

On the subject of words- she reminded herself, she had a few choice ones for Helen, before the miserable cow was past hearing them. Her lips were starting to turn blue and strings of vomit were trickling from the sides of her mouth. Glynis leaned forward and started to shout at the woman dying at her feet.

"Ostrich steam iron holy? Table knickers the coronation street, tuppence-a-head the trousers, indigo and cushions! Prawn bloody cocktail them vacuum, picture frame plumber's mate handlebars!" Glynis sat back in her wheelchair, pleased with standing up for herself at last. If that hadn't told the cow then nothing would.

Wilber loved the books so much...

By Kate Booth

Frank was overwhelmed by the size of the task. When his mother had died he had inherited this house and it was full. Generations of valued items, clutter in every in room, and loads of books. His first attempt at tidying had led to piles if books on the floor. His great grandparents' books from the 1800s he had placed gently to one side. He wanted to read them, or at least do some research but that would have to wait. First he wanted to sort the books out. The piles of reference books had collapsed into the piles of gardening and travelling books. The fiction books had been sorted into alphabetic order of the writers but he had then started making piles based on themes. Whodunits', horror, vampire stories, humour, vet stories, medical. The piles were getting smaller, but because Frank had put odd books at right angles it made some of the stacks wobble. When would Frank get the chance to dig, plant, and mow his garden, or travel to Egypt or Peru? Enough! He was drowning in this chaotic library. What could he do? Modern technology must be able to help him out. Out came his computer, and he called up Google.

-Help with sorting books   (He *didn't* want more books.)

-Shelving units?

-*No. There were book cases all over the house.*

Breathe deeply. And then the thought occurred to him!

A 20th Century machine should be available to do the job. So Frank swapped over to Amazon on the internet. The rest would be history, or at least Frank hoped by the next post. When the postman brought it, Frank named his new friend Wilber. He had arrived with his own set of tools, and an instruction book…..well Frank might read it, but he wanted to see what Wilber could do to start with, on his own.

Frank had started to talk to his new friend, so it was not so odd to hear Frank speak out his wishes and then wish Wilber good luck and "I'll see you in a week."

Frank could hear crashes and bumps for the first few days, so Wilber was obviously mobile, but then things went *very* quiet. Frank waited with baited breath until the set week, but he had not expected the sight that greeted him.

"It doesn`t look like you have done the job Wilber."

"No Frank, you forgot to plug me into a printer, so when you do that, I will get you up to speed. Job completed three days ago. So I have enjoyed reading your Whodunit category, Frank.

Good category Frank.   Best wishes, your friend Wilber.

It made Frank smile.

A Silky Special Dress

By Margaret Kerswell

She sat in the cafe, the cool air conditioning welcome in the stifling heat of the Californian sun. The friendly waitress who'd taken her order was heading back towards her with the biggest ice-cream sundae that Vicky had ever seen.

'Whoa,' she thought, things in America really were that much bigger.

Vicky settled back, spoon in hand; she loved coming to Joe's for a sundae. She had done every Thursday, when she could since she'd moved here five years previously with her mam and dad; she was sixteen years old at the time. Living in America was so different from the quintessential English market town she'd spent her first sixteen years in. She'd loved it though, she'd made some amazing friends during her time at the local high school and as she sat about to dig into her favourite ice-cream she smiled as she remembered her graduation and prom.

Happy memories of the most amazing night flooded in to her mind. Vicky put a spoonful of Joe's homemade vanilla ice-cream into her mouth and allowed it to melt, oh how she'd missed this, the ice-cream slid down her throat as soft and silky as the special dress Vicky and her mam had bought for her prom. Achieving every dream she'd ever dared to dream at Harvard University was amazing, but nothing could compare to Joes homemade ice-cream.

Cooking with the dark arts – a weekly food blog

By Martin Booth

In this week's blog I shall be looking at a problem which I know a lot of my readers have: how using magical ingredients in a kitchen can affect other, normal ingredients and utensils. Now, in a perfect world, we would all have separate kitchens for magical and non-magical cookery but for most of us this is simply not possible.

I've had an email from Witch Groody from Royal Leamington Spa. She writes: Every time I use bats wings and eels in a dish I find I have to reset all the clocks in my house, including my iPad. Is there anything I can do to prevent this? Well, Witch Groody (love the name!) I've been doing some research into this for you. It seems as though this is not a new problem, and this combination of ingredients has apparently caused problems back as far as 1178. For example, in 1794 a Warlock chef produced a dish using bats wings and eels for his local lodge in London. The ensuing chaos stopped timepieces and church clocks as far north as Stoke on Trent. Modern thinking is that the magic intrinsic to the bats wings (which is quite strong) uses the eels to slither through the space-time continuum and affect devices related to the passage of time. As an aside, I'm also reliably informed that modern physics is well acquainted with this problem and all clocks, etc. (and laboratory apparatus) are given a Hex on manufacture to safeguard it from this effect. I'm afraid that there really is no cure for the problem, but you could try a number 47 Hex over the kitchen before you start cooking and Incantation 398 over any utensils before and after use. Oh, and take your watch off.

Now, on to more serious matters. All cookery goes through fads and fashions – smears on plates, beetroot with everything and so on – and the current 'in-food' is Unicorn. This can be deep fried strips of skin as a garnish to add a frisson to a simple dish, or a whole Unicorn as the centrepiece for a banquet. Now in this blog I don't differentiate between white or black magic: each has its adherents and we all have to eat. For my own part I enjoy dishes from both sides of the magical realm and develop recipes accordingly. Similarly I will try to help all magical chefs get the best from their ingredients. Actually, in terms of ingredients, there is very little difference between white and black magic – Unicorns being an example.

Once you have caught one – and that's not an easy task, given the current availability of bona fide virgins – you have to slaughter it. Tradition dictates that the magician who captures the Unicorn must slaughter it and this is a job requiring a strong stomach. This is because Unicorns look unbelievably pitiful as you approach them with a silver knife. Creeping up behind them is impossible, as they instinctively know where you are and turn to face you. Asgrabad the Malevolent in 1601 attempted to surround a Unicorn with one hundred warlocks, each with a silver knife but his dish failed because the Unicorn appeared to face each warlock at the same time.

Once the deed is done, however, butchery is pretty standard and normal cuts of meat can be produced. In taste it is something like a cross between well matured beef and venison, rather gamey but best eaten rare. Cooking can be done in an ordinary kitchen, the only downside is the rather annoying tendency of the meat to produce multi-coloured sparkles each time it is cut or stirred. Some chefs have turned this into part of the spectacle of the dish, but for most it is merely an effect.

I have tried Unicorn many ways, but my favourite is Unicorn and dumpling stew, served with grated mandrake root, sautéed potatoes and peas.

Now, I'm not going to tell you how to make a stew… you all know that. Just remember that Unicorn needs to be cooked like beef, but quite slowly. Just use the meat as you would beef, and allow maybe an extra half hour in the oven – long and slow is always better. The only important bit is the recipe for Mandrake root sauce and please read the warning at the beginning.

Oh and you might find Incantations 22 and 943 helpful in neutralising that sparkly problem. Recite them three times before you start in the kitchen and the room you eat in. I wouldn't recommend keeping the leftovers in a plastic tub either – it will sparkle for ever! If you do find any residual sparkles, Hex 123 is a powerful cleaner spell, but use carefully. Enjoy!

For the Mandrake root sauce:

Please remember that pulling a Mandrake root is a dangerous action. If you are not protected from its shriek as it is ripped from the soil it will kill you. I firmly recommend wearing ear plugs *and* ear defenders, and wearing garden gloves as the outside of the root can irritate sensitive skins. An alternative is to tie the root to the tail of a sacrificial animal and make it run. The root will be pulled out by the animal which will succumb to the shriek. As you have not touched the root you will be perfectly safe.

200 grams Mandrake root, grated
1 tbsp White wine vinegar
Pinch English mustard
Pinch caster sugar
Salt and pepper
150 mls double cream, lightly whipped.

Take about 200 grams of root, peel well and grate finely. The vapour can be a little irritating and so should be done in a well-ventilated kitchen. Mix with the vinegar, mustard, sugar, seasoning and the cream and put in the fridge for half an hour before serving. It will keep in a sealed container in the fridge for up to a week.
Next week: Rat fricassee – Middle Ages standby or modern take on rodent cookery?

Character

By Harry Lane

And here we are. I, here, the character hidden behind the interpretation, this fool's folly. And you there, the audience, in your cinema or theatre seat. We make eye contact and perhaps in that moment you sense something more than the actor's performance. You see me, torn from the script or stage play and paraded here before many, either in the spotlight or on the silver screen.

Would you be me just for a moment, to stand inside this charade and go through these motions? To have people gape and gawk and not understand? Would you be me, would you take that step and cross over from audience to true beating heart of this character? You could always step back, I could not nor would I hinder you.

The step is taken and I sigh as I settle back into my seat. Up there before me you take my place. Uncertain at first but then you begin to settle in as the actor stamps his mark on your soul. You follow him around, smiling, laughing, crying at his command. The eyes of the others taken from that page look back. They greet you and make you feel warm for you have taken that step and now stand where they tread.

The story unfolds and you look at me, you play your part well and the others stand with you. You are not afraid for you know I will not desert you. And you now know what it feels like to stand naked and exposed, to say what you would not speak, to move when you should be still. This was the heartache we all shared, the anonymity we all bore. None knew what we truly felt, no-one heard what we had to say. The actor's parody, the anvil from which he beats and shapes his character.

Although at times alone and empty there is a camaraderie amongst us, one that is borne from shared experience. To play the hero and the villain, the King or the court jester, from all of this we are woven and from all of this we rise time and time again. Whether it be from tales around a camp fire long extinguished or verse written on dry parchment we are here.

And so my friend step back if you will for we have seen your kindness and your courage and you, have heard our song and joined our dance. Step over please and take your seat and I, my place upon the stage. And when we come and take the bow above that applause and cheer, a silver tap upon the shoulder there: "Thank you, thank you, thank you, for you have played your part".

Sleeping Beauty: A Fantasy

By Margaret Kerswell

Aurora roused with her eyes still closed and stretched. She'd had the strangest dream... but she couldn't quite remember it all. Something about buildings higher than the tallest tower of the palace and carriages which moved without horses! What kind of fantasy world was that?

She lay there a little longer still not opening her eyes, trying to remember the rest of her dream, but it was quickly slipping away. Oh well, she may as well move. Just then came a knock at the door "Come on Sleeping Beauty, you're gonna be late for work," a voice drawled. It wasn't a voice Aurora recognised; she opened her eyes and jumped!

This wasn't her bedroom in the palace. It wasn't her four poster bed, either. Where in the Kingdom was she?

Rising, she headed to the small glazed hole she assumed passed as a window and looked out. What she saw nearly made her heart stop in her chest... this definitely was not part of her kingdom!

Below were people but they were all dressed very strangely and on the wide tracks were the horseless carriages of her dream, although Aurora was quickly thinking it had indeed been a nightmare!

Just a Phage He's Going Through

By Oonah V Joslin

The sound of the surgeon's footsteps approached, click, click, along the corridor and the waiting room door squeaked open.

"Mrs Fallon?" He held out his hand and she took it. "Shall we sit down?"

"Oh dear," she said. "Is it bad news?"

"No nothing like that," he reassured. "On the other hand, I feel we may have more questions than answers here."

"What can you mean? Were you not able to remove the obstruction?"

"Indeed. However, there were several."

Mrs Fallon fidgeted nervously.

"Yes, your wee laddie seems to be a bit of a poly-phage."

"Poly-phage," she repeated.

"Yes. And possessed of a fine swallow and remarkably flexible jaws."

"Really?" Mrs Fallon had turned a little pale.

"We found a ripe apple, a whole one, slightly digested but nonetheless intact, some pink fuzzy lint, seeds, nuts and some little coloured hollow plastic balls."

Mrs Fallon showed no lack of recognition for any of these items. "And?"

"You don't seem very surprised, Mrs Fallon."

"Well I was just wondering if there was something you hadn't mentioned yet."

"No. But listen don't worry. He's going to be just fine. And children go through these phases. He'll probably grow out of it."

"Yes. Thank you Doctor," she said. "It's just -- I was wondering about our hamster."

Bigg Night Out

By Daniel Brown

It ended, like so many things in Newcastle city centre on a Saturday night or Sunday morning, with an act of violence. A few shouts, blows traded in near darkness and footsteps retreating rapidly into the night. Me, sliding down the walls of Pudding Chare with blood pouring from my left side and a piercing scream from a passer-by. For almost everyone else, that would be the last of it; a trip to the hospital, a confused statement to the police, a short paragraph in the regional newspapers and back to the same old routine of punching the clock from Monday to Friday and punching bevvied up beer monsters on Saturday nights after an afternoon spent drinking it up and watching the football. Not so for me.

I'd been watching her dominate the dance floor for almost half an hour. She used her body the way a farrier uses an anvil, letting the beats pound against it relentlessly as she threw herself across the floor with complete abandon, making shapes no human body could possibly adopt without agony, yet a slight sheen of perspiration shining under the washed out blue of the strobe lights was the only sign of any exertion. Her face was as serene as any statue.

I left my bottle of piss-water weak American beer on the bar and moved out onto the floor myself, anxious to dance with her. Not because I fancied her; she was far too angular, too *intimidating* for any of that "Do you come here often" nonsense. I just wanted to move with her, to lose myself in something that wasn't beer, or bruises or a slapper slathered in fake tan for once in my life. A Sunday morning with no hazy regrets or awkward exits from a house I'd never seen before felt like a bloody good idea.

Out amongst the gyrating crowd, I made my way into the gap of negative space surrounding her, feeling self-conscious and awkward with my typical clumsy, tentative, macho-bloke-on-the-dance-floor shoulder twitches and my arms kept firmly below chest level. No sooner had I started to shake when she stopped dancing and stared straight at me, immaculately timed with a break in the tune of course. Up close her makeup was too thick, lending her the look of one of those Chinese or Japanese opera actresses, her deep brown eyes too round and her mouth too wide to be considered at all beautiful or even pretty; the only word that could be pinned on her was "striking" and even that didn't come close to doing the reality of her justice. Her stare was haughty, confrontational; she didn't say a word, or even blink, but I knew the shape of her challenge to me: If you think you're good enough, try to keep up; show me what you've got.

The bass kicked in hard after that second-long rest and she flung herself backwards, a crab-like posture, and straightened again, her arms wind-milling in perfect synchronisation with the thumping, grimy beats. I hesitated for a half second and saw a look of contempt begin to creep into those oh so wide eyes, when the downbeat caught me in its grip. Without shame, self-consciousness or reservation, I began to dance back at her, my feet jigging furiously and arms making wild, random, yet somehow *just right* motions; I wasn't a thirty-eight year old builder's yard manager, I was the eighteen year old who'd flung himself around fields and warehouses with Ecstasy in his blood and The Prodigy in his synapses.

The songs blurred one into another, a meshing of house, techno, and grime that counterpointed the staccato pounding of my heart, the only rest coming in the fractional delay where the clumsy DJ mixed one track into another. In those minuscule silences, we would stand bare centimetres apart and stare each other down. There wasn't any lust, or aggression in those gazes; it was a hunger, the hollow need to feed off each other and the music. A feral appetite for music and motion.

I don't know how long we'd carried on in that manner, but it could have been five songs or fifty; I only know we were heading towards the exit, still dancing in our gait. Our steps carried the rhythm of the tunes still pounding in our brains. Outside in the muggy heat of Newcastle in August, we kept dancing as we wound our way through the broad streets and narrow chares, the half heard rhythms of music blasting from pubs and clubs as we passed providing our tempo. Whether it was Cascada or DJ Sammy, Mz Bratt or Redlight, or a blast of Scooter from a passing car didn't matter. What mattered was that our bodies maintained their irregular orbit, always connected by the gravity of our movements without ever touching.

The well-lit streets of the city centre fell behind us and we danced along the Quayside, the spotlights of the Baltic Gallery and the Sage reflecting off the Tyne and casting us in white and yellow shimmers as the bass from the river side clubs caught us in its grip. We slid into the darkness of the old warehouse district and the music faded away, leaving only the pumping of our veins, the rushing of blood in our ears and the hyperbeat rhythms of our hearts to keep us in time. The rushing of distant traffic formed our melody, the half heard peals of raucous laughter carried on the night air were all the vocal we needed. We skirted the city centre and danced along the Scotswood road, through Benwell and Heaton and Jesmond; across the open green expanse of the Town Moor and through the verdant, leafy growth of Ouse Burn. The city sang to us and we danced for it.

By the time the first light of the false dawn was glowing above the empty space in the east where the ship yards once stood, we were back in the city centre. We were still dancing, but the confrontational edge had gone from our movements and instead we dipped and swung around each other in perfect harmony; two bodies moving with one purpose, which I don't understand even now.

Halfway down Pudding Chare, we stopped, staring into each other's eyes from fractions of a centimetre apart, noses tilted to one side like the prelude to a lover's kiss and breathing in each other's musk, swapping breath as intimately as a sleeping couple. She smiled at me, face lit by an expression I couldn't understand. She turned and walked away from me, while I stood and trembled as adrenaline flooded out of my system.

A cool, pre-dawn breeze sighed behind me, tickling the tiny hairs on my neck and drying the beads of sweat forming in the small of my back, setting the chip wrappers and burger cartons aquiver as I watched her pirouette through the Sunday morning detritus with the grace of a ballerina practising her forms.

For the first time in hours, I heard a rhythm without needing to dance to it; the sound of footsteps approaching from behind me and to my left. I was still lost in thought, caught up in the afterglow of... whatever had happened... to take in the strained words "Please give her back." as a sharp pain blossomed all down my left side. I turned, swinging punches with both fists, acting purely on a Saturday night scrapper's instinct and saw a pale, washed out, shell of a man standing over me; realised that I must be sliding down a wall from the way he towered above my not tiny frame. I shouted something, I don't know what, but the word "mine" seems clear in my memory, apart from the times when I remember "hers". Then a woman's scream, rapid footsteps fading into the distance, maybe sirens and worried faces at strange angles asking questions I couldn't answer.

Five days have passed since Sunday morning in Pudding Chare. I write this on my sister's laptop, borrowed so that my family know what happened. Each night, the rhythm in my blood grows a little more insistent and the lights of the city outside the hospital window flicker a little more knowingly, beckoningly. I know what she is, I think, but I don't care and I don't care about my inevitable abandonment that I saw in my attacker's face; I only care that each night she dances a little closer to the hospital and tonight, Saturday night, she'll find me. Tonight, the rhythm started at teatime, when Geordie men like me listen to the football scores and make ourselves pretty for the Bigg Market after darkness falls. Tonight, we dance again and this time, please God this time, we don't stop at first light. I never knew how much I loved the city, until I saw her walking away.

Vegetable Stew

By Martin Booth

Inside the fridge, in the dark, the discussion was anything but cool. "Traditional British veg," said the carrot in a loud voice, "that's me! And another thing," it added, "I'm sooooo healthy! I'm full of carotenoids."

"You're full of something," muttered the cauliflower, sitting on the shelf above.

"Nah, that's just what he's been grown in," chipped in the red pepper. "I mean, you're grown under the surface… in the dark and stuff and I'm from another level entirely… up in the air, away from all that soil stuff."

"So that makes you better does it?" shouted the carrot. "Bloody foreigner anyway." He rolled around in the vegetable tray. "I'm one of your traditional vegetables, me. English as you like. Grown in the fine English soil in Lincolnshire."

Silence reigned in the fridge for a few seconds, then a new voice entered the discussion. "Actually, you're wrong there." Everyone turned to look at the speaker. "You're wrong," repeated the courgette, nestled in amongst his brothers and sisters.

"Wrong? Look, mate, I'm as English as roast beef and fish and chips and… and…" "Well, yes, I'll give you that," said the courgette, "but as far as been here forever? Sorry, mate, but you're like most of us in here. An immigrant!"

There was pandemonium as all the veg started arguing together, shouting at one another to make their case for Britishness and tradition. Eventually a pack of sausages could take no more. "QUIET!" it thundered. "Be quiet and let's sort this out properly." The sausages turned to the courgette. "You. Explain what you mean."

The courgette made itself more comfortable. "Right. Actually, carrot, you originated in… what is now Afghanistan, and you weren't introduced into this country until the 1660s…"

The carrot was incensed. "That has to be a lie! Afghanistan?"

"Yep. 1668 is the first record of you, mate. If you want a traditional British veg, talk to the cabbage. His ancestors were grown by the Celts!"

Fuming, the carrot turned on the cabbage, sitting quietly on a shelf. "You! Say something!"

The cabbage looked on. "Such as? Look, carrot, I'm proud of my history as a veg… and all my brother brassicas. We're the traditionalists."

The carrot, realising that he was losing the argument, went back on the attack. "Well, what about you?" he said quietly to the courgette. "Even your name is French!"

"Ah, tant pis, mon enfant. Ma coeur, c'est dans les États-Unis… I'm a squash and we all originated in the Americas. Taken to Europe and probably brought to Britain with Italian immigrants. Maybe I should 'parla Italiano'?"

All discussion was momentarily halted by the fridge door being opened. The internal light blazed on and all the vegetables closed their eyes while a large hand reached in, grabbed a can of diet Coke and retreated. Only when the door was firmly shut and the inside of the fridge was back in the cool darkness that the discussion raged on. All the vegetables were now involved, all shouting at one another about who came from where and when they were first introduced to Britain. After several minutes, everyone stopped to draw breath. It was down to the sausages to restore order before the fight broke out again. "Right then," they began, but the carrot wasn't going to be silenced so easily. "It's obvious I'm a traditional British veg," he said. "Look at me! I'm solid, tough…"

"That means 'thick' and 'chewy'," came a voice from the back. The carrot glowered but carried on. "Only a vegetable like me would really do well in this country."

"Will you be quiet?" said the sausages, patiently. "Right, we'll go round all the vegetables present and see what they know about their origins." The carrot said nothing but glowered at the rest of the fridge contents. "I'll point at you and you say what you know." They turned to the carrot. "And you keep schtum!" As the sausages swiveled round, all the veg began to explain where they were form and when they first came to Britain. "Onions?"

"Roman times, just like my pungent friend in the door, garlic."

"Leeks?"

"Same!"

"Peas?"

"Same," they chorused from the freezer compartment.

Finally the sausages looked at the carrot. "Seems as though only the peppers and courgettes arrived after you, mate," they said. "So it seems that you are a relative newbie, here in the veg rack. Even though you have become a staple of British cooking doesn't make you a long-term inmate, as it were. Bit more humility, if you please!"

There was a chorus of assent amongst the veg. "OK, OK, I get it," said the carrot. "But don't forget, everyone, roast beef just wouldn't be the same without me." For a few seconds no-one said anything. Then a very quiet voice from somewhere said. "Have you noticed that when he takes a bath he leaves an orange scum around the pan…?"

"No-one under the age of forty…"

By Margaret Kerswell

"No-one under the age of forty should be allowed to travel abroad, and that's a fact," my Grandad stated one afternoon, when we were sitting enjoying a cup of his favourite tea together. I looked up, a little shocked to be honest. The force my Grandad had used, and his tone of voice, had been strong, irritated, and almost venomous.

"That's quite a broad statement, Grandad," I replied gently.

"Well, just look at this on the news. Another young person has gone and blown themselves up, all in the name of religion," he said sounding more than a little exasperated. "In my day, there was none of this shit," he added, casting a disgusted glance at the TV in the corner.

"Granda!" I said taken aback. My Grandad never swore, not one curse word did I ever hear him use.

"Well" he said, "it's getting worse, young folk killing each other and blowing themselves up. It's a damn disgrace, that's what it is. If they stopped everyone from travelling then there wouldn't be as much of it."

"How do you know that?" I asked. "They might still be blowing themselves and others up."

"At least," said Grandad calmly, "it would be in their country, their homes and places of work! They may think twice when it's their own family and friends they were killing!"

"I guess so," I answered, "but why under forty? What about the older people who do it?"

"Most of them's youngins," Grandad said simply. "By the time they turn forty I'd expect them to have more sense!"

Good Morning, Geraldine

By Harry Lane

Geraldine stretched, yawned and stretched again. The grass felt wet and the churchyard was covered in a rainbow-hued silken dew. This was a good day for travelling. The hedgerow opposite was teeming with life – bees, butterflies, birds, spiders and even voles scuttling about among the roots. Everyone was out and about and raring to go. This is a dawn of promise, she mused.

With another stretch she was off, making smooth headway and humming to herself: she loved mornings like these. Just then, coming up behind, she heard a constant drone, drone of a familiar voice. "Morning, Geraldine," she heard as Horace the bee hove into view.

"Hi, Horace, you're looking well."

"And you're looking sleek," he laughed.

"Where are you heading?" inquired Geraldine, She liked to get the gossip.

"Oh, I think I'll just pop over the wall and into the meadow… lots of nice flowers there."

"You take care then."

"I will," he said and off zoomed Horace in the direction of the old stone wall that surrounded the churchyard.

Geraldine chuckled. She was getting up quite a speed as she went down a slight dip. It was as though she was skiing, she thought. Travelling was always easier when the grass was wet. Coming up ahead were two large stones. She slewed round them, having great fun. Another familiar sound reached her ears. It was a kind of ping, ping noise and suddenly something flew over her head and landed a short way in front.

Geraldine slowed down. "It's Freddy!"

Freddy was a grasshopper and he was sitting on a grass stem tickling his nose with his foot. "Morning, Geraldine."

"And where are you springing off to on this fine summer morning?"

Making my way to the corner of the churchyard. Maybe hang out with some of the boys."

"Enjoy yourself, then."

"You too," and Freddy disappeared in a single leap.

Once again, Geraldine chuckled, found another dip and went even faster. Then somewhere high and behind her she heard something that made her frown, a sound that did not blend in with the harmony of the morning. It was not the affable drone of Horace but a sharper zap, repeated again and again. It was the type of sound that came with a lightning storm.

"Well, hello there." A voice like breaking ice on a pond. It was Zachary Pleb, the wasp.

Her frown deepening, Geraldine replied," Good morning, Zachary."

He was definitely the most unpopular creature in the churchyard.

"And where are you off to?" More ice breaking.

"Just starting out," said Geraldine.

"I've been on the go for a while," said Zachary.

She ignored his sarcasm. "You?"

"Just patrolling. Well, I can't stay to chat." Zap, and he was gone. Geraldine heaved a sigh of relief – thank goodness for that.

Carrying on her way, Geraldine felt much more comfortable and relaxed, slowing down her pace and just gliding along. *Whar whar whar.* Geraldine smiled, she knew who this was, coming up behind her like a miniature helicopter. Stopping, she turned and saw, settling next to her, Bert the Ladybird. Bert was her favourite, bright by colour and fun by nature. He was laughing – Bert was always laughing.

"Top of the morning, Bert. Going far?"

"Just cruising, enjoying the sunshine. And you?"

"Mmm, pushing forwards, getting there and travelling fast." Geraldine gave a throaty laugh, a twinkle in her eyes.

"Not bad for a snail!"

Forever Berries

By Oonah V Joslin

Red patent leather winks out from the central window of the store. On the left uniformed dummy-girls wear pleated gym slips, bound with fixed girdles of red or green or blue. One is uncomfortably bundled up in an unseasonable Burberry. On the right, boy dummies in short or long trousers, blazers with badges, segmented caps and stripy ties look unrealistically clean. Satchels and socks, berets and scarves, too neatly strewn on the floor, little resemble the real world of a child's bedroom. Homework haunts the back lot of my dreams but in the theatre that is the shop window, those red patent shoes hang ripe on my mind. I would hint at liking them but hints need to be carefully staged and subtly delivered not to earn a smack. Instead each time we pass, I look and love at a tantalising distance with feet that long to dance.

This time of year the greengrocers has punnets of this and that -- jewelled fruits with hidden juices and exotic names -- not quite forbidden but scarcely affordable. I rehearse their names; apricots, plums, damsons, cherries, grapes.

"Four of each today?" the man asks, meaning oranges, apples, pears. He serves them into brown paper bags and my mother hands over her wicker basket.

"I'll take a punnet of strawberries too," she says, "and two bananas."

"Well, if you're feeling flush, the cherries are just nice for eating."

"How much?"

They wink at me -- shiny like the shoes.

"Well, go on then. I'll take a wheen."

He weighs a 'wheen' like sweeties on the big scales. "Sixpence, a shilling, two bob…"

She's feeling flush. I might just mention those shoes… Wrong decision. My leg smarts.

Later in the playhouse, I prepare privet salad with rowan berry tomatoes, bits of clay for meatballs and wee potato stones; I set the plate in front of my doll and give her a cup of nice clover leaf tea. She remains expressionless -- *ungrateful* child.

There's a cherry on top of the condensed milk on top of the fruit salad, for tea. My sister smacks her lips.

"Mind -- there's a stone in that," says Mammy, and gives it to me. Maybe by way of an apology for the smack.

So I nibble away the flesh and it tastes like… It doesn't taste like anything at all. Just sweet -- like any other piece of fruit; only not like strawberries taste of my birthday and not like grapes taste of hospital, not like dates and tangerines taste of Christmastime. Disappointment lingers unspoken on my tongue.

In the store they measure my feet and bring a pair of sturdy, black, StartRite, lace-up shoes. The assistant undertakes the unfathomable task of cross-lacing and tying.

The red patent shoes have a little button on the side, a little red button with a white eye that stared at me on the way in.

"Those are a bit dearer than I planned," says my mother, feeling for my toes inside each shoe and probably regretting the cherries.

"She's a double EE width fitting," explains the assistant.

They look at me as if it's my fault.

"Take a wee walk," says Mammy.

I march up and down the thick carpet and dare not say I don't like them for there is no choice and one of others will have to have cheaper shoes.

"Are they comfortable? Remember you have to walk all day in them. Will we take those?"

I nod my head and on the way out, carrying the box, I don't look in the window at the reproachful patents shining on their stand. They are not for the likes of me, with broad feet and narrow prospects, but still they've hung on my heart for all these years -- like all the people I can never be -forever ripe and elusive as the taste of cherries.

If only…

By Martin Booth

If only we'd paid more attention… The detonation had been forecast – anticipated – for decades, but when it eventually happened it surprised watchers the world over. The first we knew was a silent blossoming of light, small at first from our vantage point but then it rapidly increased, growing bigger and brighter. It became clearly visible to anyone who cared to look up into the night sky, until it outshone the full moon.

Daytime watchers could see it clearly, too, marvelling at how it could still be seen even on a sunny day. For three weeks the brightness increased until, one morning, it began to fade – the show was over. Six hundred and forty light years away, the star Betelgeuse had ceased to exist, blasted into cosmic dust, gas and radiation.

The doom mongers predicted the usual, of course… end of the world, rain of comets, aliens. The more radical churches and sects were making noises about since Betelgeuse had been a red giant it was the gateway to hell. If we'd have been closer it might have been, bathing the Earth in radiation from its death throes, but we were safe on that score.

Some sky watchers said that the supernova had destroyed habitable planets in the sun's 'Goldilocks zone' and that we should mourn for the extinction of life and civilisations. Perhaps.

For the most part, though, people enjoyed the celestial show and laughed at the theories over their coffee or Chardonnay. The more knowledgeable recognised that Orion would look different now – the constellation would have a glowing nebulous cloud for its shoulder, not a neat single point.

When Betelgeuse exploded, six hundred and forty years ago, what would the mediaeval monks have made of it? A sun being destroyed by God's wrath for wrongdoings? If only we'd paid more attention to their ideas…

If only we hadn't laughed…

Maybe we'd have known better how to deal with the survivors…

Cyclops, Maze, Pandora's Box

By Margaret Kerswell

Tobias paused and looked attentively around. His heart was racing but he knew he needed to push on. Carefully he adjusted his belt and then picked up his highly polished shield and spear. He had to do this and he had to do it now. Why, oh why hadn't he brought someone with him, and then they could have been a distraction for the cyclops who was the guard to the entrance of the maze? Hindsight was a great thing though, and Tobias hadn't, so he'd just have to run hell for leather and hope he made it.

Another quick look told Tobias now was as good a time as any and he started to run....he ran as fast as he could with his heart pounding in his ears so loudly he thought his head might explode.

He made it as far as the maze entrance and paused, once again looking around, expecting at any second the large club of the cyclops would fall, but it didn't. So after taking a second or two to pull himself together Tobias stepped forward in to the relative coolness of the maze.

That was when he heard it. The sound started low and grumbling at first but it quickly rose to a high animal like howl. Tobias ducked down and spun around, trying to look everywhere at once. Where in the name of the Gods was the sound coming from? He had no idea he turned quickly to head further in to the maze when suddenly he knew what had made the sound, as stood before him was the thing he'd been avoiding... The cyclops!

The cyclops was at least twenty eight feet tall and as wide as a house (or at least that's how he looked to Tobias)

"Oh hell" muttered Tobias.

Daniel was the third generation of cyclops to guard the entrance to the maze and he hated his job. Most days it was boring at best and on the days it wasn't boring it was simply mind numbing. He'd come into his post after some sailor had caused his father a misadventure five years previously. He'd been eighteen at the time and now at twenty three he was, to be quite honest, ready for a change.

This morning though he was even more glum than usual. He'd slept in, meaning that he'd had to wolf down his three sheep and two goat breakfast, to the dulcet sounds of his father berating him. "You'd never catch me late, thirty two years on the job and I was NEVER late, NOT ONCE! You've been there FIVE years, FIVE measly years and look you're late already, bad time management that is…" There was probably a lot more said, but to be fair Daniel had simple switched off, eaten his breakfast and left.

As if breakfast hadn't been bad enough, when Daniel had let himself in through the back door of the maze, the stupid thing had swung shut jamming his fingers, causing him to cry out with pain (this had been the sound Tobias had heard) and now to top it all off he'd just stumbled upon this human starting to make his way in to the maze, no doubt looking to steal Pandora's Box. Daniel stared down at the human; he was fairly muscular, although he'd still be no match for Daniel himself. However Daniel simply didn't know if he had the energy.

"Go away," Daniel shouted at the man.

"No," came the response from Tobias.

Daniel drew himself up to every bit of his twenty eight feet and growled "Leave now or I'll crush you!"

"Oh no you won't," cried Tobias as he quickly ran passed the cyclops's legs and into the maze…

Once passed the cyclops Tobias took the right-hand corridor, praying he'd made the right choice as he ran on.

The corridor was long; it was dimly lit by lanterns burning with a naked flame spaced regularly along the walls, the flickering lights giving the long corridor an eerie feeling to it.

Tobias ran on. He could hear the cyclops shouting behind him. All of a sudden he noticed a gap to the left of the corridor and he ducked in to it.

Tobias stood stock still, back pressed against the hard, cool stone wall trying as hard as he could to control his breathing as he listened to the steps of the cyclops, getting closer and closer...

Daniel was annoyed with himself; he couldn't believe he'd let the small human pass him so easily and now he'd lost him in the darkness of the corridor. If his father found out about this his life wouldn't be worth living... his head ached at the thought of it.

Near the end of the flame-lit corridor Daniel paused. Where had the human gone? Daniel was sure he couldn't have gotten that far, his legs were way shorter than his own. Pausing and catching his breath Daniel suddenly spun around as he remembered the small recess in the left of the corridor.

"I wonder," he muttered to himself as he walked back toward it.

He didn't really want to hurt the human, just scare him enough so he'd leave then Daniel could get on with his day in peace.

Maybe he'd even ask the human why he was there. Oh, he knew it was for the box - it was always for the box - but Daniel couldn't understand why. I mean, why would anyone or anything want the manky cobweb covered thing anyway? It truly was beyond Daniel. But he was curious to know so maybe if he got the chance he would ask the human to tell him.

That is if the human didn't escape again!

Tobias stood listening as the heavy footsteps of the running cyclops pass his place of refuge and moved further into the half-light. Slowly and quietly he let out a long breath, his heart was pounding in his chest and he could hear the echo in his own head.

Then suddenly the footsteps stopped, all was quiet apart from the jagged breathing from both Tobias and the cyclops.

When the footsteps started again it took Tobias a few seconds to realise they were coming closer.

Quickly and quietly Tobias placed his shield and spear on the floor of the maze, he then carefully and methodically started to feel around the walls of the dark recess where he stood, trying to find an alternative exit, or a space he could crawl into to hide. At the very least he wanted to make it difficult for the cyclops to get hold of him.

With the sound of footsteps getting closer, the feeling of cold, hard unyielding rock under his finger tips and the threat of being crushed still ringing in his ears, Tobias started to pray...

As Daniel passed the last flaming torch before the recess he took hold of it and lifted it from the cradle. He knew the recess was dark and he didn't want to risk the human escaping again. He wanted to talk to him. He had questions, he was curious and he wanted answers.

As the darkness within the recess started to recede Tobias froze. His mind was in overdrive as he tried to remember the exact position of his shield and spear. Why had he placed them down? (He was regretting it now). Slowly Tobias turned and came face to face with the cyclops.

For a few seconds Tobias and Daniel just stared at each other, mentally assessing the situation. Daniel definitely had the upper hand here, as his huge bulk meant that escape past him out of the recess was basically impossible.

Tobias's eyes drifted for a split second to the large studded club which Daniel held effortlessly by his side, they then flickered over to where he'd laid his shield and spear. Why, in the name of the Gods, had Tobias ever thought putting them down was a good idea? His mind raced once again as he considered making a break for them…

Daniel noticed the human looking at his club and then at his own discarded weapon. It was then he decided to speak.

"Don't panic," he said. "I don't want to hurt you."

"You don't want to hurt me?" questioned Tobias. "You said you were gonna crush me!"

"True," said Daniel, in the gentlest tone he could manage. "But I only meant to scare you a little."

"Well, consider me scared," responded Tobias shakily.

"Look," said Daniel, trying to maintain the same gentle tone. "It's me job you see, when folk try to come in here and take that manky old box. It's me job to stop them. It's nothing personal, you understand?"

"OK," said Tobias. "But you got to understand, when someone says they're gonna crush you, well it's kind of hard not to take it personal."

Daniel considered what the human had said and slowly nodded his head.

"I guess I see what you mean," he said slowly. "Look can we start again? Forget about the crushing stuff," he added.

"Emmm, you want a do over?" questioned Tobias. Daniel nodded his head. "We can do, I guess, so how we gonna work this? You gonna shout at me to leave, obviously leaving out the crushing stuff and then give me a ten second head start?"

Tobias swallowed quickly before the bile rising in his throat escaped him. This was it, this was the end. This hulking twenty-eight foot cyclops was going to finish him off, he thought.

"What we're gonna do," said Daniel, "is get acquainted properly."

He stuck out his large hand, somewhat nervously.

"Hi I'm Daniel," he said gently.

Tobias couldn't help but chuckle to himself. Stood in front of him was 'someone' who was a good twenty two feet taller than he was and Daniel (as he now knew his name to be) was also at least three maybe four times his breadth. Tobias guessed that he could probably eat him for a snack if that's what he wished, yet he looked and sounded nervous. 'Go figure' he thought and held out his significantly smaller hand towards Daniel's.

"My name" he said clearing his throat "Is Tobias, and it's erm nice to meet you, I er guess" he said feeling nervous himself.

"So," said Daniel, standing up straight, "what now? I'm guessing you still want that mouldy old box?"

"Yes," Tobias replied, "I do. It's not for me really though, but for my village. We need its help, if you know what I mean?"

"Not really," came Daniel's response. "I've always been told it's a bad thing. That's why it's in the maze - why three generations of my family have guarded it. You know, to stop bad stuff happening."

"Some things are worse than what that box could do, trust me," said Tobias a little wryly.

"You reckon?" asked Daniel.

"Yes, I reckon," said Tobias. "I've seen some first-hand," he added.

Daniel wanted to ask more but one look at his small companions face with its grave expression told him it may be better not to.

After a few seconds Daniel spoke again.

"OK, Tobias, if it means that much to you, I'll help you."

Tobias looked up at Daniel. "You'll help me?" he asked quietly.

"Yes," came Daniel's reply. "But, if I do this I'm finished here," he paused as the magnitude of what he was about to suggest started to sink in. After a second or two he continued. "Yes, I'll be finished here. My parents will disown me and there won't be a cyclops for miles who'd welcome me. I'll be a disgrace to me people." He stopped and cleared his throat. "But to be fair, I hate this job anyway, so if you're willing to let me come with you, then I'll help you."

"You'll help me?" Tobias repeated still sounding surprised.

"Yes, I'll help you. I'll guide you safely through the maze to the manky box you seek and I'll guide you out again, safely," he finished.

Tobias stood stock, still processing what Daniel had said. This was a big thing for him and Tobias was quite taken aback at the offer. But having this hulking great cyclops by his side would definitely be a big plus in the journey that lay ahead of him.

"Well?" prompted Daniel, "what do you think? We got a deal?"

"Yes, if you're sure?" Tobias said as he retrieved his shield and sword. "Then yes, I'd welcome your company on this quest."

"Come on then," said Daniel "This way…"

Wood shed live

by Oonah V Joslin

Mouse had been outside foraging and came back all excitement and fuss. He had news he couldn't wait to tell; so much so that his whiskers were twitching and his tail just wouldn't behave. It ripped right through the mend that spider had just made in her web.

"No consideration!" spindled spider.

Mouse took no notice. He didn't understand spider anyway. She spoke a little too quick.

"Where have you been all this time, Mr Mouse," his mate scolded. "You were gone so long, I was worried!"

"Never mind that. I'm back now, and I got what you wanted." He dropped a nice bit of bread in front of her. She was pregnant again and he knew she was fond of a nice bit of bread. "But oh, Mrs. Mouse," he spluttered, "you'll never guess!"

"No I won't," said Florrie Mouse, "and most likely never know either unless you calm down and tell me, Mr. Mouse."

"Fox told Sparrow and he told me, those people who were here last year filming the cubs have set up cameras right here in this shed. We're going to be on TV!"

Florrie immediately began grooming. "Oh Mr. Mouse for shame -- and look at the state of me! All fat and bedraggled."

Toad was Zen about winters. Winters made him lethargic and really one didn't want to do too much other than breathe in and out. Mostly he slept. The rest of the time he pretended to be asleep but he was conscious of almost everything going on around him.

"T V you say? Cam-er-as?" he croaked in his slow drawling voice.

"Yes. Fox told me. Isn't it exciting?" affirmed Mr. Mouse, skittering around.

Toad really wished mice wouldn't do that, it was exhausting. "I hope they get my best side," grunted toad. He was an ugly old devil but he had his vanity.

"You have a *best side*?" said Florrie settling down.

"And there you've gone and ruined my lovely web!" spider complained, frenetically trying her best to repair the damage. "I may have to begin it all over again."

"What's up with Spider?" asked Mr. Mouse.

"Says you wrecked her web with your tail," said toad very deliberately.

"Didn't mean to. Tail takes on a life of its own at times. Please do apologise to her for me, Toad."

"Says sor-ry," Toad told Spider.

"Oh well I expect I shall have to manage. Maybe I can make an even better web for the cameras."

"Don't know why you'd bother," chipped in Armadillo Vulgaris. She and her friends had gathered in a puddle in the corner beneath the leaky the roof and were drinking water with their bums – a neat trick common to all wood lice. "Probably don't like spiders anyway."

"That's where you're wrong, AV," Spider said. "There are lots of arachnid fans out in TV land and even when they don't like spiders, most humans appreciate webs – it's both and art and a science, you know and I am told *they* have one as wide as the world!"

"I still don't see what all the fuss is about," said AV. "I mean TV? I ain't never seen TV!"

"Oh but I have," said Mr. Mouse. "I got into the house once and the humans were watching this little box much smaller than a shed yet it had a whole world inside, bigger even than the garden."

"Well, I never," said toad.

"And Fox told Sparrow that because people had watched him on TV, they actually feed his cubs for him these days instead of chasing them off."

"Well then, you never know, AV," said Toad, "maybe some of them could even think you absolutely charming and not stamp on the next woodlouse they see! Anyway, I like you. In fact why don't you and your friends come over here and let me see how pretty you are?" He gave a low, toadish laugh and flicked out his tongue ready for action. "Now," says he "where's that camera?"

The Ring

By Linda Jobling

The year was 1921. I was created from the finest emerald from Burma with two large diamonds from South Africa. Most of the rings in Mr Morgan's shop were second hand, sold to him when times were hard. Mr Morgan would polish me every day, before putting me in Tray 9. He often admired me and used to say, "This is the most beautiful ring I have ever made".

It was a warm sunny day when a young soldier and his girlfriend stood outside the window. He was dressed in a brown khaki uniform, his buckle, brass buttons and artillery badge gleaming in the sun. His back was as straight as a die, with his arm linked to the beautiful young girl. She looked radiant in her bright yellow flowery dress blowing lightly in the summer breeze. She was petite with long auburn curly hair, held in place with a yellow band, and a small flower on the side. They stood there for a while deep in thought and looked at each other.

"I really like that one, the one with a green emerald and two diamonds on the side. Yes that's the one I would like," she said. "Remember tray 9 no.66."

I think they have chosen me.

They made their way toward the heavy oak door to the side of the shop.

"Look Ivor there's a notice on the door: 'Gone to lunch – back at two o'clock'." Ivor looked at his watch. There was still time before the last train.

I watched in horror as I saw the disappointment on their faces as they made their way to the Copper Kettle on the other side of the street.

I prayed they would come back.

"Can we have a look at that emerald ring you have in your window please, Mr Morgan?"

Mr Morgan took the ring from the window with his scrawny fingers, partly covered with fingerless gloves, and gave it to Katherine to try on. A perfect fit.

Ivor had saved most of his pay for the last year, and was hoping he had enough in his wallet.

"We'll have it please" he said

I was in a beautiful red leather box with a silk lining that had 'Morgan's the Jewellers of Newton', printed in gold on the lid.

That night he slipped it on Katherine's finger, then carved a heart with KH and IP 1921 with his penknife on the tree, and proposed to her. "We'll get married when I'm back on my next leave in a few months' time" he said

The day of the wedding was a beautiful hot summer's day. Katherine sat on the hay cart on an old carved oak chair, covered with wild roses, in her mother's wedding dress. It fitted her perfectly. On her head, she wore a handmade Victorian lace veil. She had meticulously gathered wild flowers from the farm and made her bouquet with honeysuckle, wild roses, ivy and wild irises.

John, her brother, had been busy all morning, brushing and washing Josh the horse, putting ribbons in his mane and tail. It was a job to get Josh to stand still, but he did enjoy pulling the cart.

Katherine sat and smiled as her brother gave his command for Josh to start trotting. He trotted along with his head held high and his ribbons and mane swishing in the breeze. Mrs Jones and her brood and Mrs Davies from the railway cut waited at the bottom of the hill to put a rope across the road, hoping John or Katherine would throw a few pennies to them as they passed.

At the Wesleyan Chapel, she was greeted by her bridesmaid looking radiant in a yellow chiffon dress with a headband made of wild flowers.

Ivor slipped a gold ring next to me and repeated the words, "I do."

I spent a whole year on the farm, next to the gold band when Katherine milked the cows, fed the sheep, skinned the rabbits, feathered the chickens, salted the pigs and cooked the bread. I was so happy then.

I can still feel the coldness of that brass bed when Katherine gave birth to her first child Florence and when there was no longer a grip and her hand fell helplessly to her side.

I remember the feel of the silk at the side of the coffin when they her carried on her last journey at the age of 21 years. Ivor took me and the gold band and put us both back into our boxes: we were never to be together again.

I have no recollection how long I was in my little box and on Florence's 18th birthday I was given to her as a present. To start a new life again.

A Bit of Bad Weather.

By Oonah V Joslin

There was a bit of bad weather if that's what you'd call it. Weather in terms of Cairn-colpagh means relative rainfall – rainfall relative that is to the wettest place on the west coast of Ireland. This wasn't a relative of anyone's. It was a whole new family of precipitation. It was bucketing down, or rather bucketing sideways with hail that hurt and drops that rivalled a pint at the Harp & Hand. Then Grogan says I'd better get in the lambs.

'Why me?' says I. I was talking to the Almighty but Grogan thinks he's on equal terms so he answered.

'Because you're the shepherd and I'm needed here for the milking if you not come back.'

'Comforting' says I. Sure enough I was the shepherd but only part time – only when the lambing was on and then he laid me off 'til spud gathering, stingey auld fart.

So I tuk Pad the sheepdog wi' me an' headed for the top lonin which was the last place I'd seen the flock. Only there was neither scrap nor tail o' them and the entire hill had been deleted from sight by the downpour. All I could do was follow the sound of bleating and hope I wasn't swept into a drain or stream for there were that many gullies. A man could sink to hell without being missed – until it was spud time anyway.

Rain lashed my face and the bleating seemed to be getting farther away and all of a sudden I was standing knee high in water in sparkling sunshine and there not twelve feet away was a leprechaun – no I swear on my mother's life – it was a real fairy-folk-person-thing dressed all up in green and with a red cap. Luckily I had my blackthorn staff – a genuine shillelagh – and I held it diagonally across me for the wee folk don't like the blackthorn, so it's said.

Now we'd startled each other so we had. I don't think he intended for to be caught out like that with a big salmon in his hand.

'And who might you be?' he pipes up.

Now I am not stupid. I know the tricks of fairy folk and I wasn't telling this wee brat my name.

'Well now, let me see,' says I. 'I'd be the rightful owner of that fair, big fella of a fish you've got in your hand from the Colpagh.'

'And who's to say it's your stream?'

'I guess that would be me again. Who's asking?'

'If I am to have the privilege of introducing myself' he said, 'I like to know to whom.'

'We appear to have reached a bit of an impasse, you and me,' I said.

He looked at me blank.

'A stalemate,' says I.

'I've an idea. I'll grant you three wishes for three fishes,' suggested the wee fella, 'and then we'll be free to go our separate ways. What is it you want? Choose careful now, 'cos a man only has three wishes in one lifetime.'

Of course I thought of wealth beyond avarice. I even thought California but then you see, I'd miss the sheep and the sweeping hills. I'd even miss the rain. It's all I know.

'I only want what I came for – to find my flock, safe and well,' I said.

In an instant I was standing right amongst the sheep and they looked as pleased to see me as I was to see them – if a bit soggy. Pad was wagging his tail. 'Pad auld fella,' I said, 'I must be mad. I'm sure even as a dog, you think so. But do you know, I wish all this really *was* mine, you, the sheep, the hill,' and I patted his head. 'And I wish this soddin' rain would stop!'

And it did! It stopped that very moment and the sun came out and when I got back down to the farmhouse and got the lambs safe, Grogan announced that he was making a few changes and wanted to concentrate on the dairy and how would I like the high ground and the sheep for my own. 'After all,' he said, 'you've looked after the flock for years and you know that hillside better than anyone and maybe it's time you settled down and got yourself a wife and a couple of wee lambs of your own.'

So that evening I went back up the cairn. There's a spot I love to sit and look at the view out over the ocean, weather coming in from the west. The sunset was magnificent. It had turned the sea to molten gold. 'This'll be a fine spot to build on,' I said to Pad. And up pops the leprechaun.

'Was this your doing?' I asked.

'You had three wishes,' he said, 'and you only used one and it wasn't gold -- so I just kept listening a while.'

I pointed to the view. 'Ah well there's some things better than gold. The real gold's out there.'

'Tam,' says he, 'you're a good man and there's not many.' And he disappeared.

'How'd you know my name Mr. Leprechaun?' I shouted, 'Am I not to have yours?' But he didn't reply and I was content with that. Somehow I thought it wouldn't be the last time I met him.

Magma

By Martin Booth

Magma looked at his watch and sighed. He was employed as a night watchman at the building site on Queen's Drive, where a new shopping mall was being built. As a troll, he couldn't really expect to get anything other than menial jobs, although – for his species – he was relatively bright. Still, he thought to himself, only four hours till dawn and he could go home. He was glad the whole 'turning to stone in the daylight thing' was only a story: Magma actually quite liked the sun warming his stony body: he was very fussy about personal grooming and carefully shaved off his moss at least once a year.

Since all the supposedly 'mythical' creatures had 'come out' two years ago, people were finding that trolls, dwarves, elves and so on were becoming more common in everyday life. Oh, there had been the usual problems with the 'Keep Britain Pure' crowd, but it was amazing how quickly any difficulties melted away when faced with six trolls and a goblin…

No-one was really sure how things had happened. One day elves were only to be found in story books, and the next they were on the bus next to you going to work. Many previously mythical creatures (or PMC's, as they liked to be called) suddenly were just, well, there. The Daily Mail, of course, blamed PMC immigration for all sorts of evils from shortages of cabbages to the forthcoming lunar eclipse, but on the whole life for everyone got better.

Magma sat on his reinforced stool and looked at the building site. He was proud of the new mall… he had seen it from the foundations up and now they were starting to fit out the shops. Admittedly the developers had had to put all the shops for trolls on the ground floor to save re-engineering the whole building and installing industrial lifts and hoists, but no-one really seemed to mind.

Suddenly, Magma heard a noise from somewhere in the supposedly empty building. "Bloody dwarves," he muttered, slowly getting to his feet. "I throw them out again." Magma walked slowly but remarkably quietly for a troll along the main thoroughfare until he could pinpoint the source of what sounded like digging. It was coming from a unit earmarked for an up-market Elf boutique. Magma shone his torch in through the newly installed window. No-one was there, but he could still hear the digging. Magma wasn't the sharpest stone tool in the drawer, but even he realised that it should take more than a shovel to dig through several feet of solid concrete. He turned off the torch and crept through the open door. Then he saw them in the back room: four dwarves, carefully making a big hole in the floor. Magma knew dwarves were strong, but to break through all that concrete in one night was extraordinary.

"Oi! What youse doin' in my buildin' site?" Magma said in his deep, gravelly voice. The four dwarves jumped at the sound and the picks and shovels clattered to the ground. One of the dwarves looked as though he might be walking home rather stiffly, too.

The tallest dwarf stared at Magma's leg and then looked up at his face. His beard was a deep fiery red to match his hair, cheeks and nose. "We are, er, investigating a leak!"

The other dwarves glanced at one another, then nodded furiously. "Yes," ventured one of the others. "A gas leak. Could be very nasty, you know. You should clear the building, now!"

Magma scratched his head, which made a sound like stones being scraped past one another in a minor earthquake and dislodged a shower of sand. He peered down at the dwarf. "No gas." The dwarf swallowed hard and joined his friend in walking strangely. Magma looked into the hole. "What you doin'?"

The red dwarf's shoulders drooped. "I can see we cannot fool a troll of your magnificent intelligence," he said. "We are on a quest."

Magma knew about quests – his mother had told him about quests in the olden days when elves and dwarves went on long journeys to fabulous places to find gold. He shook his head. "No gold here. I seen the floor. Just soil and stuff."

One of the other dwarves tried to explain their presence. "Look, er, troll, do you know what a bank is?"

Magma nodded. "Yes. People put their money in it to keep it safe."

The dwarf continued. "Well, there's a bank here in the mall and we are paid to test how safe it is."

Magma frowned as he processed the information, then slowly nodded. "I see. So you is security, like me!"

The red dwarf looked very relieved. "Yes, yes, we are from bank security, testing the strength of the vaults underneath us. So you see, there *is* gold here. Now, troll, you have done a very good job in discover… er, checking on us, but we need to finish our work here."

Magma still felt that something wasn't right, but he started to turn round. Then he stopped and turned back. "Youse will put all the stuff back in the hole, won't you?"

"Yes, yes, of course. Oh, and don't say anything about this, will you. We are security, after all."

Magma walked slowly out of the shop and back to the site hut, leaving the dwarves to pick up their tools and attack the floor again. One of them started to quietly sing "Hi ho…" but was hit with a shovel to dissuade him from going any further.

Back at the hut, Magma sat and thought about the dwarves and their quest and gold and banks. Trolls didn't use banks, much. It would be a very stupid robber who decided to steal from an irate eight foot tall being made of igneous rock. He knew something wasn't right and in the end Magma decided he had to find out whether the dwarves really were security or were just up to no good. He stood up and pushed open the door to the site manager's office. It was locked, of course, but that didn't matter. Magma carefully unrolled the plans for the mall and looked at the ground floor. The elf boutique was about half way along the mall, and Magma's finger eventually found it. Then he looked at the plans for the basement. No bank, just a deep underground car park. Magma scratched his head again, then brushed the sand off the desk. He was about to roll up the plans when his eye caught sight of the layout for the first floor. There, right above the boutique, was a branch of the new PMC Bank plc. It took a few minutes for the penny to drop for Magma, but when it did he held his sides as he laughed.

Down in a hole in the elf boutique, another of the dwarves heard (or rather felt) Magma's laughter and, thinking there was an earthquake, began to stand awkwardly. The red dwarf hit him with a shovel, and they carried on digging. "S'gotta be here somewhere. I've seen the plans."

The fourth dwarf stopped hitting the bedrock with his pick and leaned on it. "Where'd you get those plans from, anyway?"

The red dwarf looked at him. "I got them from a vampire bat I met in the pub."

The dwarf looked at him. "You moron! How do bats spend their days?"

The fourth dwarf hit the red dwarf with his pick just before three goblins, wearing blue lights on their heads, appeared at the top of the hole accompanied by a smiling Magma.

He looked at the three conscious dwarves and grinned. "See, I knew youse wasn't security. You thought I was a stupid troll, but at least I know up from down!"

Extracts from the Pages of the Dark Lord's Confession

By Daniel Brown

I really can't believe you expected my answers to fit in those tiny boxes in the first place. However, I've complied with your wish that I write all of my previous answers down *yet again*, but this time with even more addenda for the clarifications you requested. Is this to be my punishment? Endlessly rewriting the same answers to the same silly questions? If so, can't we just skip to the show trial and then have me hanged. It must be better than this tedium.

1. Grishnabolg Lundkovskyi, Emperor of the East, Lord of the Black Lands, Master of the Eleven Schools of Sorcery, Architect of Destruction, Bringer of Hellfire, Archduke of the Volcanic Lands of Lysolt, Journeyman Blacksmith (second class).

2. Not paying proper attention to an idiot farm boy with an ancient artefact.

Addendum to 2. What, the truth isn't good enough for you? Fine! Being "evil". Apparently subjective judgements of one's moral character are enough to warrant being zapped with bolts of magical energy, illegally extradited and imprisoned, these days. And genocide. Pointy eared little shits had it coming.

3. Some farm boy with a ludicrous haircut.

4. I don't remember the exact time. I was too busy being zapped with a bolt of ancient magic. Ask the floppy haired fop who discharged it.

5. Really? You want to know what I was doing prior to my "arrest"? I was going about my business being an "evil emperor". You know the sort of thing, ordering villages burned to the ground, having female prisoners oiled and brought to my chambers, evil rites of black magic, oppressing people, lurking malevolently in corridors, that kind of malarkey. What do you think I was doing? I was doing paperwork. Do you have any idea how much paperwork goes into administering the empire? Of course you do, you're making me fill out this ridiculous form. My memory is bit hazy, due to the above mentioned bolt of ancient magic, but if I recall correctly I was signing an order that declared all farmers in the empire be educated about crop rotation. Hungry people are a bit rubbish at expanding an empire.

6. I don't remember. As stated above, I WAS ZAPPED WITH A BOLT OF ANCIENT MAGIC! No matter what you were doing beforehand, that tends to loom large in the memory. The bloody great zap of magical energy has driven every other memory from my mind. So far as I know, the sequence of events went as follows; Paperwork, paperwork, paperwork, some farmboy with a ludicrous haircut saying something about the nasty rain being finished or something, bolt of magical energy.

7. What sort of question is that? Don't you think if I'd been aware that some twit from the back country was going to come and zap me with the Phylactery of Whatever the Hell it Was, I might have taken a few precautions?

8. No. I deny the charge in the strongest possible terms. It's just a tool. You might just as well charge an innkeeper who makes a bowl of soup you don't like with "engaging in acts of black cookery".

9. You're not catching me out like that. I've never used "black" magic.

10. It depends on how you deprive depravity.

Addendum to 10. Is that all it takes? In that case, yes. If that boggles your minds, try the Jhendari Mouth Organ.

Further Addendum to 10. [Redacted by clerk of the court, for the sake of modesty]

Further Addendum to 10. Ask your wife.

11. Is that rumour still doing the rounds? What was I supposed to do, starve to death? How was I supposed to know that help was on the way?

Addendum to 11. That doesn't mean they were looking for *me*.

12. They had it coming. Those trees weren't doing anything where they were and I needed masts for my naval fleet. Just because the empire was landlocked at that time, didn't mean it would be landlocked for ever.

Addendum to 12. Yes, all of them. I've got better things to do than look over my shoulder for pointy-eared, big-eyed, tree-huggers bent on vengeance.

13. Of course not. If I went around slaughtering entire generations of children every time some smelly old woman declared this one or that one to the Chosen This, Prophesied That or Foretold Other I'd rapidly run out of new recruits, wouldn't I?

14. Yes. Does this facility have security measures? Of course it does. I'd be foolish not to have security measures in my own castles and fortresses.

Addendum to 14. I think it was rather ingenious, myself. It's not everyone who can create a castle made entirely out of fire, levitate the whole thing 100 feet in the air and then man the walls with the souls of the damned.

15. A little bit.

Addendum to 15. 100,000 infantry troops, 35,000 cavalry troops, 5000 war machines and their crews, 500 Dragonriders, plus the various supporting people necessary for an army of that size. It's not the size of the army that matters, but the fact that none of it was my fault.

Further Addendum to 15. It's not my fault they chose to stay there. I told them we were passing through there on the way to the Great Eastern Ocean. They could quite easily have moved.

Further Addendum to 15. Well I moved almost a quarter of a million people there, didn't I? And yes, I believe 30 days notice was more than adequate notice for evacuating an entire country.

Further Addendum to 15. It was a very small country.

Further Addendum to 15. All they had to do was get out of the way for a couple of weeks, then go back to their lands and lives, get out of the way again for a couple of weeks during our return journey, then go back home again and just carry on as normal; with the exception of paying one quarter of all national income for the nice new highway I built for them.

Further Addendum to 15. Yes, the ground trampled by my passing army counts as a highway. It was lumpy before we arrived, flat after we'd passed through. Highway.

16. How dare you? They aren't "abominations" as you so crudely call them. They are creatures, like any other. You just need to get to know them a little better. And be imprinted on them when they first leave the spawning pit. It probably helps if you're naked when you deal with them, as well. Don't know why, but they all seem to hate when people wear clothes. Must be an error in the combining spells. Still, you can't get everything right, can you? Once you get to know them, the Winged Bears are lovely. That being said, perhaps in retrospect we released them into the wild too soon.

Addendum to 16. It could be far worse, we could have released them in a *cold* country. I also think it makes for an excellent incentive for the people of Rhylosia to remain fit and in good physical condition. The Winged Bears almost never attack a naked person, unless they're hungry or the person annoys them or wasn't imprinted on the Winged Bear in question when it was spawned.

17. I refute that claim and resent the implication that worshipping the self-proclaimed God of Evil makes His followers evil by default. People who worship the God of the Rivers don't go around drowning all the time.

Addendum to 17. Well, yes; they did in my Empire. That was entirely unavoidable.

Further Addendum to 17. They couldn't breathe underwater.

18. I don't know what a coterie is, so possibly yes, possibly no. Is it a group noun, or a particularly large number, or something?

Addendum to 18. Oh, I see. Yes and no. I kept a harem, but no one was there by force, coercion or any other kind of compulsion from me or my minions. There's a certain type of person who gets fixated on powerful people. I thought it best to keep all of them in one place. Safer for everyone else and safer for them. Despite how this tribunal is trying to portray me, I'm not a monster.

Further Addendum to 18. Not really. The harem was self financing, thanks to my steward being ingenious enough to think of charging people for tickets to watch.

Further Addendum to 18. The fighting which inevitably broke out between the crazy women who all thought I was their soul mate.

19. Absolutely not.

Addendum to 19. Once again, no.

Further Addendum to 19. For the last time, no. I did not, have not and never would build a weapon of mass destruction. I built a sophisticated territorial defence spell, on account of the unjustified aggression shown by my Empire's neighbours.

Further Addendum to 19. Of course it was defensive in nature. You don't think I'd unleash a spell like that unless I was threatened, do you?

Further Addendum to 19. Well dozens of neighbouring nations and the first alliance of Men, Dwarves and People Who Might be Descended from Elves Several Generations Ago (See question 12 for details) in almost 1000 years looks pretty bloody threatening to me!

Further Addendum to 19. Only because building the Spell of Ultimate Defence was expensive. That sort of thing doesn't come cheaply, you know.

Further Addendum to 19. You all could have just paid and all of this would have been avoided.

20. Really? You put that question on this form? Very well. The heart of a 17 year old virgin girl, lightly toasted.

Addendum to 20. I was *joking*. Just whatever is being made will be fine, thank you.

POSTSCRIPT: If "whatever is being made" could be delivered by a 17 year old virgin girl, that would be wonderful.

POSTSCRIPT POSTSCRIPT: Also, a brazier and a skillet. Many thanks.

You will all pay for this infamy. My vengeance will burn worlds, etcetera etcetera, so on and so forth.

Signed Grishnabolg Lundkovskyi, Emperor of the East, Lord of the Black Lands, Master of the Eleven Schools of Sorcery, Architect of Destruction, Bringer of Hellfire, Archduke of the Volcanic Lands of Lysolt, Journeyman Blacksmith (second class).

Bursting Bubbles

By Kate Booth

I loved the way she said "Balloons". She said it as if she were blowing bubbles, with her lips puckered. She was so beautiful, but so vulnerable. I had first met Maisie at Phil's party. She had been sitting curled up on a sofa, all alone.

"Hi, you want a dance?" Just a shake of her head. No luck there.

"Do you want a drink? Phil's made a crazy punch."

"You have got to be joking" she replied but had a wry smile on her face. "What's your name? I'm Maisie, but take my advice, **never** drink One of Phil's potions."

"I'm Ian and I'll stick to the bottled Newcastle Brown."

We settled in to a really relaxed chat. She wasn't one of the Uni. Crowd, but was training as a Nanny. My archaeology course was rather stodgy, until I told her about finding the tiny leather shoes buried in the mud. I was amazed that talking about ancient children lit her face up.

"They used sheep's bladders to blow up as balloons." I said

"Ugh. That must have tasted horrible. And it must have gone mouldy."

"Don't panic. They pickled them in vinegar or something. The small bairns were looked after by wet nurses anyway, so the Ladies of Leisure didn't have to get sheep's bladder on their precious lips." There were no drinks that night, except from the cold tap in the kitchen. We agreed to meet at the park the next day, and she arrived pushing a Silver Cross pram. They walked for a while and then settled on a bench.

"You could make a living doing that kind of thing." She laughed, and said her only problem was sorting out who to work for. I heard how her training took on a circuit round various families, so she got to meet children of different ages, and parents of different "character". Today's little tyke was Paul. Three months old, his mum was still on maternity leave, but this was his first whole day away from her. He gave Ian a long hard stare and waited.

"Hello little man, my name is Ian, give me a smile." Ian smiled, but Paul just kept on staring and his bottom lip began to tremble.

Maisie distracted him for a moment by singing a sliding note, from low to high. When she had his attention she spoke his name, and praised him for being a good boy.

"Do you want a smooth balloon?" And a sharp snapping sound came from under the pram. Baby Paul didn't jump but Ian did. It was right next to his hand, and it was just like a trick that his big brother used to play on him. Maisie turned to Ian and realised that he wasn't very happy. She reached out her hand, and touched the back of his hand. She smiled when he looked up and was so pleased when he relaxed, and put his hand over hers.

"Do you have any tunes you can hum? It has a magic effect on Paul" Ian shook his head, and went back to watching Paul. "I'm so sorry I made you jump." She pulled up the end of a red balloon from her other hand. When Ian and Paul were both watching she let go of the end and let it snap. And this time she had smiles from both of them and nobody jumped this time.

"Balloons are much more fun when you blow them up."

Maisie lifted the end of the red balloon to her mouth and blew hard into its redness. After the first blow, she gathered the end, held it up and made the balloon wobble. "Is that big enough? Or does it need another puff?" No reply from Paul but Ian broke into a broad grin. After taking a deep breath in Maisie blew slow and hard into the end of the balloon. Another puff went in, and Maisie held up the balloon. It was round now, and she swayed it, side to side. "It's as big as an apple, but we can't eat it. Let's have some more puffs in here." Maisie held the end of the balloon tightly in her lips. She forced another two puffs in slowly. Each breath was drawn from deep in her chest, and her eyes were watching Ian, who was watching her. She holds the end of the balloon tight, and sat back to inspect the progress. "Not bad, not bad."

Maisie held the balloon near Paul, who waved his hands so they bumped into the growing red balloon. It made a slight thumping noise, which he liked.

"Big enough?" purred Maisie, her eyes smiling at Ian this time.

Ian thought of the sting of his brothers' prank all those years ago, and resolved not to let it spoil this fun. "You decide Maisie; you seem to be the expert."

Maisie went on smiling. "A little at a time, and keep checking there is enough to tie off at the end. It would be a pity for it to *explode*."

Her eyes were wide as she changed the tone of her voice; checking that the baby was ok with the drama in her voice. Baby Paul just went on smiling.

"Wasting a balloon, and all my hot air." Ian caught the change in Maisie's smile, and the rakish glint in her eyes, and he said "Well let's see the expert at work." And that's what Maisie did, more breaths, and the balloon grew huge.

)**BANG**(They all looked surprised and jumped up from their seat on the bench. They were laughing, even baby Paul. "Wow, that was huge when it burst, but my dress is stuck to the bench." Her hand had reached down to the back of her skirt. There was a nail in the bench that had hooked the fabric, and this was now torn.

"Can you free me Ian?" There was quite a long tear, so Ian tried to keep Maisie decent. He took his sweat shirt off and tied it round her waist.

The top of the nail had quite a firm grip on the fabric so Ian had to pull and twist to unhook it. He gently ran the back of his hand down her thigh. "No injury?"

"No, I'm OK thank you; but can you get rid of the strip of torn fabric? It hangs down like a tail."

That was more of a challenge; so they agreed that one yank would look less inappropriate.

>**Rip**< Ian stood up bearing the strip of Maisie's dress, and had a really broad grin. Maisie laughed and ran her hand down the rip in her dress. "You do realise Ian, that Dresses with slit seams are now the most fashionable and expensive items in the shops at the moment."

"But let me help you replace the dress. I don't think it will give the right impression.

"You've got a deal, but I have a spare balloon."

Up came her hand holding a Pink Balloon!

So that was the start of Ian and Maisie's romance.

Worship me!

By Martin Booth

"Why aren't you worshipping me, mortal?" The figure drew himself up to his full height.

"Not interested, thanks."

"But I am a GOD," he thundered. "I have powers unimaginable to mere mortals... I can destroy worlds and create havoc in the Universe."

"Really?" I said.

He fixed me with a hard stare. I wasn't terribly impressed. "Would you destroy me?" I asked.

"Of course," exclaimed the god. "You doubt me?"

"No, no, but..."

"What?" shouted the god. "No buts!"

"Well, no disrespect," I said with a smile, "but it's very hard to respect the 1 cm tall god of woodlice."

A Moment's Reflection

By Emma-jane Anderson

"Sit still, Lizzie, make the most of it before we have to start walking again." I slowly soak the rags in the water and wrap them around my sister's tiny feet. I look up again to check on mother. She has been standing on that bridge for quite awhile now. I hadn't heard much of what that woman told her about father at that last house but she has barely said a word since. Father had left that village months ago. The lady wasn't sure where he had gone and everything after that had been whispered, probably so Lizzie and I wouldn't hear.

I return my attention again to Lizzie. She has no idea what's going on. She was only 2 when father left to find work. I doubt she even remembers him most of the time. She doesn't remember how angry he was or how often he would leave mother sobbing when he took the last of mother's jug money. I don't know why we had to follow him - it's been 3 years. I don't know why mother stopped working for Mrs Harris. It may have just been a small room but we were happy there and I'll be 12 soon and I'll be perfectly capable of finding work.

I finish covering Lizzie's feet. "Does that feel better?" Lizzie nods, her red cheeks streaked with dirty lines from crying. "Stay there and rest. I'm going to check on Mother."

I'm not sure mother even knows I'm there until I speak. "Did she even know where father might have gone?" She turned silently and looked at me: blank, far away eyes not really seeing me, just pointed in my direction for just a moment before returning to glance at the rushing water below. "The boys at the last village said there are lots of pits and they are always looking for people. If father isn't at the next one maybe I can get a job. We don't have to tell them my real age. We could use the last of the money from Mrs Harris to get a room. Mother?" This time she didn't even look at me. She just continued to stare into the water.

"Bring Lizzie to me."

It had been the first thing she had said for hours. I ran over and scooped up my sister up and began carrying her to mother. "Are we walking more?" she whined. "It's been days, I don't like sleeping on the outside." It had been days and I understood why mother had not wanted to use the last of her money for travel. She didn't know if father had suitable lodgings for us and she needed to keep hold of as much as possible. It had been 6 solid days of walking to get to the village he had been at last year, when mother last heard from him. Goodness only knows how much further we had to go now, but at least we were moving again.

Mother took hold of Lizzie and held her tightly by the arms. She sat her on the side of the bridge and placed her hand on my cheek. I watched as she took a deep breath. Then I watched as her eyes finally saw me. She blinked and looked at Lizzie who was swinging her legs. She lifted her down and grabbed her hand. "Better make a move, we've still got a long walk. Jack get the bags."

Lara's Big Day

By Dave Telfer

The nurse hurried towards Lara's bed. She was having a bad dream again. Nurse Cameron sat and stroked Lara's head until she had calmed down.

"Same dream, pet?"

Lara nodded, her shoulders still shuddering from fright. "It was horrible, just like being there again. When will they go away?"

"Shh, I'm sure they'll stop soon. After all, you are due to get out again next week and then you'll be home with your family again. That will be nice for you, won't it?"

Little Lara lay for a while, thinking about that terrible day when she and her family had been out for a drive. But before they got to their destination a van veered over the central reservation and ploughed into the car she was in. Her Mum and her Dad had escaped with cuts and bruises but the back of the car, where she and her brother had been, took the full force of the collision. Her brother had been thrown clear and suffered a broken arm and three broken ribs. He had been released from hospital some time ago.

Lara had not been so fortunate and she had received a fractured hip and severe injuries to her right leg, sitting as she had been behind the driver's seat.

Lara dozed off with the nurse still gently stroking her forehead, a sad expression on her face.

Next day, the patient was taken up to practise again using the temporary prosthetic limb she had been wearing for the last three weeks. The surgeon had said that she was lucky that they were able to amputate below the knee, as that had made it easier to adjust to her new limb.

"Well, I told you that you would be walking by your eleventh birthday, didn't I?" The friendly giant of a man smiled down at her. He was very pleased with her progress. It hadn't been easy for the little soul.

"Well, I still have five days to go," replied Lara. "I hope you haven't told anyone?"

He leaned down, and said in a conspiratorial whisper, "Not a word. This will be your big surprise, Lara. I'll see you tomorrow morning and your new leg will be ready for you to try out. How does that sound?"

Lara didn't reply, just squeezed her shoulders together and gave a big, radiant smile that melted the hearts of everyone present.

Five days later, Lara was bursting with excitement at the imminent arrival of her family and her grandparents.

"Is it time yet?" she asked Nurse Cameron.

"Almost. Ah, come on, here they come to fit your leg."

The team worked swiftly fitting her leg, then sat her in an easy chair by the window, a blanket over her knees which reached down to the floor.

At last she could see her parents hurrying down the corridor towards the ward, the others close on their heels.

"Happy Birthday, Lara." Her Dad reached down and hugged her, followed by the rest of the family. They started handing out the packages, but Lara stopped them and asked them to stand back a little.

"I have something to show you."

Lara pulled the blanket away and slowly, carefully, stood up. The family were stunned into silence. Then she walked, slowly and carefully, over to her Mum and Dad and gave them a big hug. There were floods of tears from everyone. Even Nurse Cameron and another nurse, on hand in case of any mishaps, were crying openly. Eventually, when everyone had settled down, Nurse Cameron led Lara gently back to her chair.

"Just a little at a time, young lady," she smiled.

Lara then opened present after present and finally came to her brother's parcel. She smiled at him and he leaned towards her. "Hey, kid, I knew you'd need them sometime, but not this soon." He grinned knowingly and nodded at her to open it up.

Lara's eyes opened wide with delight.

"Goody! Two shoes!"

Author Biographies...

Emma-jane Anderson:

My background is as wide ranging as my writing topics, from performing arts to psychology, visiting several places in between. I've always enjoyed writing, finding it a great escape from reality. Saying that, my main interests lie in real people and their experiences. I find people's stories fascinating and believe they should be documented and shared with future generations.

Daniel Brown:

From the minute my parents gave me a junior edition of Robinson Crusoe within a few months of my learning to read I've loved stories. In fact, I loved them a little too much and took to telling outrageous whoppers to anyone and everyone who'd listen. One day in Primary School a kindly teacher sat me down for a quiet word. He explained that if I wrote my gigantic fibs down on paper they weren't lies anymore, they were stories and I couldn't get wrong for them. It was called 'being a writer' and it was OK to be one. In fact it was one of the best things a person could try to be, according to Mr Ross. I was sold. I've been telling outrageous lies ever since and because I put them down on paper I hardly ever get wrong for doing it. How cool is that?

Harry Lane:

I began writing at school during free periods and lessons such as Comprehension. I gained great pleasure from this and found it very rewarding. However, after leaving school and starting work, I just got out of the habit of writing. After I retired and had more time on my hands, I joined this group of welcoming and like-minded people and realized what I had been missing. I have once again regained the pleasure and satisfaction of Creative Writing.

Kate Booth:

I'm a blissfully happy married Mum of three amazing grown-up kids and grandmother to two. I have worked in hospitals and then became a secondary school science teacher. Sadly in about 2003 I was diagnosed and having MS and took early retirement. As a naturally curious and enthusiastic person I have valued being so welcomed into the Pegswood Writing Group. I had never really experienced "writing" before, but it has given me a way to express difficult ideas and to cope with my MS problems. I try not to get depressed – I just write.

Martin Booth:

I am a retired Science and IT teacher who spent many years writing worksheets for school but little for myself. Towards the end of my career I started to create exemplar material for the pupils (which amused them and confused senior staff). The Creative Writing Group has allowed me to discover a style of writing which permits me to explore some of the stranger and darker aspects of life. It is more interesting, after all. I have also been accused, (quite rightly, as it happens) of leading my fellow writers along dark paths.

One of those paths has included following Margaret down the publishing route, and 'Santa, Aliens and War' is the result. Writing, like all Art, should engender discussion and allow people to form opinions – at the end of the day, though, I write for me and my own enjoyment.

Linda Jobling:

I have always been interested in the stories my Grandfather used to tell me from an early age, and when I saw a Creative Writing group in Pegswood, I decided to join and record some of my childhood memories and stories. I have learnt a great deal and feel privileged to be a part of a very talented group of writers and poets.

Margaret Kerswell:

As a mother of three boisterous boys I don't always have a huge amount of time to myself. I use writing as a bit of an escape and a way to cope with life events and experiences. I think in rhyming couplets so I tend to write rhyming poetry or verse! Joining the writing group at the Hub has encouraged me to try different ways of writing and subject matter. I always find my fellow group members to be encouraging and supportive, especially when I decided to put some of my poetry together in a book and so The Juicy Duck and Other Poems came to print. When the idea of a collaborative publication, where all the proceeds went directly to the Hub arose, we all agreed that we'd love to be part of it. So here it is… enjoy!

Oonah V Joslin:

Oonah Joslin's book is called 'Three Pounds of Cells' because that is the weight of the average human brain, but since her brain is still inside her skull it's difficult to tell whether it's underweight or overweight to match the rest of her. Scientists (and many other people) can barely wait to find out. Oonah hopes to keep them guessing for a long time to come, though you can take a peek inside the book any time you like. Oonah lives in Pegswood and Cyberspace where she edits The Linnet's Wings and writes the odd post in Parallel Oonahverse.

Dave Telfer:

All my connections to the arts started when I was 14 and wrote my first song and started a vocal quartet soon after. I did gigs as an impressionist which led to a skiffle group in the late fifties. In the Sixties I had a folk band and organised many junior performing arts groups. In the seventies, among other things, I wrote a rock opera. The Eighties was more of the same. The Nineties saw me organise the making of 3 music videos, starting song writing and co-founded a music association. The Noughties saw my involvement in writing, attending several writing courses and groups. I wrote a book and a pantomime.

Pegswood Community Hub

Pegswood Community Hub is an independent community development charity that has been working in Pegswood for over twenty five years. It provides a creative, safe, friendly and stimulating environment for community activity and support.

The main goal of The Hub is to create a sense of community in our village where people live and work. We hope that an increased sense of community will lead to more people being involved in our cultural, educational and social activities, which will create a better sense of folks supporting one another.

The Hub, originally known as Pegswood Open Project, was originally based in a small colliery house on the terraces, running mainly family based activities and eventually groups for the wider community.

By 2001 the activities had grown to such an extent that larger premises were being sought and we were fortunate enough to purchase and extend a large building which met everybody's needs.

A number of improvements were made to the building such as having a community kitchen fitted which gets used weekly; and a computer suite with 12 computers which are available for all to use.

In 2016 we celebrated our 25th year in the village and we are still going strong.

For more information about what we do on a weekly basis and all our special events please see our website:

www.pegswoodcommunityhub.org

Printed in Great Britain
by Amazon